THE COMPETENT
AUTHORITY

Iegor Gran

THE COMPETENT AUTHORITY

*Translated from the French by
Ruth Diver*

MOUNTAIN LEOPARD PRESS
WELBECK · LONDON & SYDNEY

Originally published in French as *Les Services compétents*,
in 2020 by
P.O.L. Éditeur

First published in the English language in 2023 by
Mountain Leopard Press
an imprint of
Welbeck Publishing Group
London and Sydney

www.mountainleopard.press

9 8 7 6 5 4 3 2 1

© P.O.L. Éditeur, 2020
English translation copyright © Ruth Diver, 2023

The moral right of Iegor Gran to be recognised as the author of this work has been asserted in accordance with the Copyright, Designs and Patents Act, 1988

Ruth Diver asserts her moral right to be identified as the translator of the work

All rights reserved. No part of this publication may be reproduced, stored in any retrieval system, or transmitted in any form or by any means, electronically, mechanical, photocopying, recording or otherwise, without the prior permission of the copyright owners and the publishers

A CIP catalogue record for this book is available from the British Library

ISBN (HB) 978-1-914495-55-7

This book is a work of fiction. Names, places, events and incidents are either the products of the author's imagination or are used fictitiously

Designed and typeset in Haarlemmer by Libanus Press Ltd, Marlborough

Printed and bound in Great Britain by
CPI Group (UK) Ltd, Croydon, CR0 4YY

This book is supported by the Institut Français (Royaume-Uni)
as part of the Burgess programme

I

The first thing that strikes the lieutenant – the woman's laughing eyes.

After three long rings, she has opened the door. The operative curtly informs her of the search order, thrusting his foot against the doorjamb to stop her from shutting it, you never know, just an involuntary professional reflex.

She shows no panic. Quite the opposite: a wide, a much too wide smile.

"Do come in!"

They crowd awkwardly into the entrance hall of the communal apartment, introduce themselves, show their I.D. cards from the Committee for State Security, recite the words of the warrant: "By virtue of Articles 167 to 177 of the Criminal Code…"

The woman scrutinises the six intruders as if she were examining the specimens in a collection of coleoptera. There is unfeigned curiosity in her eyes. Amusement, even. Although she realises that, at this very moment, her life is collapsing into a ghastly series of troubles and tribulations, she still cannot help feeling a delightful dizziness. A gambler's excitement.

"I didn't quite catch your name, lieutenant. Speak up, would you? What was it now?"

"Ivanov. Evgeny Fyodorovich Ivanov."

The lieutenant recites his full name and tries to find an inconspicuous spot near the coat rack. Not a chance! The woman's grey-blue eyes follow him.

"You're a bit tense, aren't you? Dearie me! How old are you?"

The lieutenant pretends he didn't hear that. As if he would ever answer such a question! That's preposterous. They're the ones who do the asking.

Captain Nikonovich, the most senior officer, attempts to take things in hand again:

"I have the honour of informing you that your husband is presently detained in our offices."

That should shut her up.

The woman can scarcely stifle a giggle.

"What a relief! Thank you, Captain. I was worried, you see. He should have come home after his lecture, at midday. He's three hours late. It's never a good sign when your husband is three hours late. You can't imagine how worried I was. What if he had been in an accident? What if he had gone home with another woman . . . ? You don't ever go home with another woman besides your wife, do you, Captain?"

She says this with such a mixture of sincerity and baffling impudence that the captain feels himself completely decomposing.

"Citizen Rozanova, Maria Vasilyevna, married name Sinyavsky, by virtue of Articles 167 to 177 of the Criminal Code, I invite you to voluntarily hand over to the investigating organs all manuscripts, publications and books in your possession whose contents are anti-Soviet."

His solemn demeanour has no effect on the woman whatsoever.

"Anti-Soviet contents? Here, in our home? Did you hear that, Iegorushka? How dreadful!"

In his little cot, Sinyavsky junior, aged nine months, sits up, woken from his nap.

"Note that in the report!" Nikonovich tries to bark. "Citizen Rozanova, Maria Vasilyevna, claims to possess no forbidden manuscripts, publications or books."

"We'll see about that." Lieutenant Ivanov grimaces, thinking he'll recover some face.

"Come with me, Evgeny Fyodorovich," the woman orders. "Here, take the baby while I make up his bed again."

When he realises what she expects of him, the lieutenant lurches backwards, but the woman is too quick for him. Whoosh! She has already picked up her son, plop! Iegorushka is now in the lieutenant's arms. What is this tornado?

Maybe she hid some manuscripts under the baby's mattress, the lieutenant thinks. We mustn't forget to have a good look under there.

In the meantime, the search has begun. It is 3.30 p.m. There are so many books in this room! An entire wall from floor to ceiling is armour-plated with a huge bookcase. Not a free centimetre anywhere! Papers and newspapers poke out from all the cracks, there are piles on the floor, under the table, under the bed, everywhere. The lieutenant feels a blend of admiration and terror. It'll take ages to read all this stuff!

But then he remembers that Lenin's personal library

consisted of ten thousand books, a fact he learned on a visit to the great leader's last residence in the Lenin Hills.

He also thinks about *Quiet Flows the Don* by Mikhail Sholokhov, our great Soviet writer – which he has never managed to finish in spite of his wife's nagging.

The ant-like labour begins. Examining each volume. Time flies! At 8 p.m., it's already dark. They've hardly even started on the bookcase. And there's another room too. How are you supposed to make any progress when this woman is always distracting you with her indiscreet questions, her inappropriate comments?

"Do you have any children, lieutenant…? What size trousers do you wear…? You should buy them a bit tighter around your belly… How old were you when you first started losing your hair…? Is it hard to get into K-Prep, the K.G.B. training school…? Do you have to know how to shoot with a pistol…?"

"We'll start again in the morning," Nikonovich orders, exhausted. "Maria Vasilyevna, we will have to close this room off because it is still in the process of examination. However, you do have the right to take what you need for the night. You have access to a second room in this communal apartment, don't you, in the basement? Shmakov, check she isn't taking anything important. Kulakov, seal off the door with seal no. 5."

They have to move the baby's cot. Shmakov and Kulakov set to it.

"You didn't search under the mattress," the woman says, still smiling. "No, no, I insist! Come on, now! Do your job. I wouldn't want you to get into trouble with your bosses on my account."

They are hesitant, embarrassed, so she offloads her son into the lieutenant's arms, and strips the bedding from his little cot in front of them.

"It's fine, it's fine, Maria Vasilyevna," Nikonovich pleads. "You must be tired… And we are too… It's been a long day…"

They leave at last, their hands blackened with book-droppings.

Once the door closes, the woman's smile fades. The son, who hadn't uttered a peep all day long, starts screaming. "I never saw him cry so much in his whole life," she would say later. "He was choking."

Next day, same thing.

The lieutenant had conducted enough searches in his career to realise that there was a disturbing imbalance here. The woman was too relaxed. The child – too calm, almost switched off. A team of removal men would have sown more confusion and caused more anxiety than the Competent Authority – despite agent Shmakov's sinister glare, which was intensified by his indigestion.

There was something odd about it all.

In the course of two exhausting days, our operatives had found nothing significant to sink their teeth into. No obviously compromising manuscripts. However, we did seize quite a few books in French. Including a copy of *Bonjour Tristesse* by Françoise Sagan, and of *Nadja* by André Breton. A few novels published by the Parisian émigré publishers Y.M.C.A. Press. A copy of *La Pensée Russe*, the Parisian émigré weekly. A copy of *Doctor Zhivago* by Pasternak, in Russian, published in Paris in 1964. Incomprehensible poems typed on a typewriter, with no author's name.

All these items were meticulously added to the list of confiscated documents. But let's be honest, a search of the home of any liberal professor, including from the science or law faculties, would have gathered up a similar, if not more abundant harvest. Is there a Muscovite intellectual who doesn't have a *Doctor Zhivago* hiding at the back of their bookcase?

The meagre collection did not tally with our expectations. Where were the screeds of anti-Soviet prose? No trace of foreign currency either. Nor any luxury goods: not a single gold coin, no fur coats. If that Judas had sold his motherland by publishing his writing in the West, he certainly didn't make a fortune on the proceeds.

When he gets home, Ivanov can't stop ruminating. Larissa cuts his introspection short:

"You shouldn't be talking about your job at home. It's forbidden by the regulations. You should know better."

"I'm not divulging any secrets," Ivanov protests. "I'm just asking you, as a woman, what you make of the psychology of this citizen, who obviously doesn't feel the slightest apprehension about the search."

"It's just that you don't look very frightening, my bunny rabbit. Even when you put on your serious, official airs, any woman can tell you're just a sweetie inside."

"I'm not vicious, that's true." Ivanov laughs. "But tell that to Shmakov, with his killer's mug."

Over dinner, a concoction of sliced spuds and cubed beef all simmered in an abundance of fat, he does get an idea:

"Ah! If only we hadn't taken so long to track Sinyavsky down… Then his wife wouldn't be acting so arrogant, that's for sure. To think this case has been going on since 1959… It has damaged our credibility."

Larissa clears the table:

"Do you remember how young we were in 1959? We'd just got married."

But the lieutenant is not feeling romantic.

"It's no wonder she thinks we're blockheads. You can't blame her. We didn't do a good job. Six years, nearly seven… That's what I always say to Kulakov: don't be afraid of recognising your mistakes. Be honest – with your mates and in front of your mirror! When you calibrate yourself strictly, I mean constructively strictly, that's when you make progress…"

Before falling asleep, Ivanov wonders whether he should mention this to Colonel Volkov from senior staff management at his next opportunity.

———

In the apartment turned topsy-turvy as if by an earthquake, citizen Rozanova releases a flood of tears, then engages in similar self-criticism. She could have had more fun. Embarrassed them by asking questions about the Ogre. That Captain Nikonovich, who at the end of the day had the cadaveric complexion of someone who had inhaled too much dust – what were his thoughts about 1937 and the great purges? That little Lieutenant Ivanov, who could have been efficient and dangerous if he hadn't been so uncomfortable with a baby between his paws – what was his experience of de-Stalinisation…? It could have been such fun…

But let's not get carried away. The aim is to disorient them gently, not to rankle them. Also to lull their vigilance to sleep. Appear to be amiable, slightly batty. Yes, amiable. They're so used to people being terrified and breaking down. Make them lose their bearings. Faced with this unsettling giddiness, they'll do everything they can to keep matters brief. And they will make mistakes. They are only men, after all.

The proof is that it works. That enormous wall of books – the operatives worked hard at it, examining each volume one by one. Without noticing, under their very noses, a metallic rod of a purely decorative appearance on the vertical support. The ornament conceals discreet hinges. You just have to pull the shelf of dictionaries towards you, while lifting it up slightly, to hear a click! and then the bookcase opens. A little camouflaged door! Behind the wall of books, a narrow space has been fitted out. Absolutely invisible. There's even a miniscule bed wedged in there, along with a pull-cord lamp and a storage area that is much better provisioned with radioactive books.

Sinyavsky likes to go and hide in there whenever a pest drops in unannounced. His wife, who is in charge of opening the front door, exclaims "Ah, who's this I see…? Welcome!" (That's the agreed signal.) The scholar joggles the dictionary shelf, and, with his stomach pleasantly knotted by this conspiratorial act, disappears into his lair. He can read there in peace until the nuisance goes away. A real caveman!

II

The lieutenant was right: when you think about it with hindsight, it is inconceivable that the most Competent Authority in the world should have taken so long to solve the puzzle. If they had only known that the affair would take on these proportions... Starting with a scrap of an article, published in France in a journal called *Esprit*. A gob of snot.

February 1959... Six months previously, Ivanov completed his training at the prestigious K-Prep. His marks in physical training were disappointing, but he is good at French, does alright at surveillance, has a lively mind, a generous memory, solid technical knowledge (microphones, cameras) and, especially, an excellent rapport with informants, what they call "enquiring empathy".

At the Lubyanka headquarters, he shares a tiny office with Kulakov, who also works in the eighth directorate, dealing with anti-Soviet propaganda.

They only have one typewriter between the two of them. "Don't complain, it's new," Colonel Volkov said. "You'll just have to learn to type faster." It's German and hardly ever jams up, even at high speed: an Erika with a Cyrillic keyboard.

The fact that the Soviet Union, this industrial colossus, can't be arsed to produce a typewriter seems to worry nobody at all: these prosaic weaknesses mean nothing when you're a cosmic power! Sputnik is worth all the typewriters in the world. "Earth's first artificial companion created in the land of the Soviets!" That front page of *Pravda*, now turned a nasty yellow because of the poor-quality paper, has been stuck to the metal filing cupboard in the corridor for the past two years.

Ivanov keeps a few red and blue enamel Sputniks in his desk drawer, along with an old paring knife he uses to sharpen pencils. A good start to a collection. These commemorative insignia will be his son, whenever he finally makes up his mind to be born. On which front there is no news for the Ivanovs at the moment. So much the better, in a way: he is free to stay late at the office.

For there is plenty of work to do.

One morning, at the weekly coordination meeting, the investigator, Lieutenant-Colonel Pakhmonov, passes round a thick book-sized journal, with a large red E stamped on its white cover.

"This was sent to us by our contacts in Paris. Beginning on page 335 is an article that is causing quite a stir in intellectual circles over there. It was apparently written here, by one of us, anonymously, and taken out to France in secret. It's called *On Socialist Realism*. All yours, Ivanov. Figure out what it says. Your French is up to it, I believe. Apart from '*bonjour*' and '*Louise Michel*', I don't have the vocab."

Ivanov gets started right away. He has always considered himself to be gifted at languages, and could have applied to the prestigious Institute for Foreign Relations, the diplomat factory, if he had been better at writing essays and quicker at maths.

His accent is remarkable. He doesn't roll his Rs as you do in Russian. A little vanity he developed at K-Prep, where he trained in the language laboratory, on a Nagra, the first portable reel-to-reel tape recorder with a crank-handle winder. Colonel Vorontsov would make the marvellous thing spin, filling it with French radio programmes.

Sous le ciel de Paris
S'envole une chanson,
Hmm hmm…

In moments of depraved reverie, instantly repressed, Ivanov nurtures the prescient idea that one day, if he applies himself and remains morally irreproachable, he might get a posting to the land of Louis Aragon and the Paris Commune… There has to be some higher purpose to his guttural R, whose depth would be a credit even to Edith Piaf.

"Rrrr…" Ivanov sometimes says to himself. "Parrris… Rrrrealism…"

On Socialist Realism is prefaced with an introduction by Jean-Marie Domenach, the editor of the journal.

"The text of which we here present the French translation is an unpublished article by a young Soviet writer, and no doubt the first critique of official academism to reach us from a Russian author living in his country. On reading it, one will soon understand why it could not be published in the U.S.S.R., and could only appear in France under the precaution of anonymity."

So, no author's name. No translator's name either. Not

the slightest indication of its provenance. No comment on the identity of the "mule". The journal has switched off all the lights – that very fact is disturbing. Usually French journalists can't help showing off. As soon as a scrap of evidence against the Soviet Union turns up, they make a mountain out of it, and blab on and on. They delight in telling you exactly where, when and how they met their correspondent, and even if they sometimes embellish things, they candidly supply nice little bits of string that you just have to pull at to unravel the whole tangle and take the necessary measures.

Nothing like that here. The absence of clues does not bode well.

Now then, what are the contents of this fire ship…? Strapping on his best French, Ivanov sends up a silent prayer to the French Communist Party leader Maurice Thorez and sets out on the exploration.

It's a jungle of thirty-five pages, with sometimes convoluted sentences and quite a few difficult words, such as "causality", "animism" or "inherent", which you have to hack into with the machete of your dictionary.

The meaning (or rather the silhouette of the meaning) does, however, finally appear. And comes as quite a surprise. The anonymous author says nothing about the Gulag, nor censorship, nor economic collapse, nor the Party elite, nor the repression in Budapest (still quite fresh), nor the strike ban in Soviet factories, nor the closed borders, nor even the contradictions of Marxist-Leninist thought or its limitations. Not a single controversial subject is raised. Instead, it's a treatise on aesthetics. Socialist realism, the major genre in which all great Soviet novels have been written since Gorky, in which canvases are painted and stone is sculpted, gets kicked in the guts with a disagreeable, sarcastic tone.

It's all rather puzzling. The anonymous author has gone to the trouble of juggling abstract concepts over thirty-five pages, then taken the huge risk of getting his writing across to the West – to what end? To explain socialist realism? Not likely! Everyone here knows exactly what it is.

In fact the author starts by quoting the Union of Soviet Writers: "Socialist realism is the basic method of Soviet literature and literary criticism. It demands from the artist a truthful and historically concrete representation of reality in its revolutionary development. Moreover, it must contribute to the task of ideological transformation and education of workers in the spirit of socialism."

"Truthful", "historically concrete representation", "revolutionary development": Russians don't really need any of these reminders. All this is taught to them from their earliest infancy. They have socialist realism in their blood. Western readers, on the other hand, may have cause to wonder. Which tends to indicate that the article was created for the West, *on purpose*. A case of premeditation, then.

You might be thinking that none of this shambles is political. But Ivanov is no fool. He can sense the irony when the author pretends to be in raptures: "The modern mind cannot imagine anything more beautiful and splendid than the Communist ideal. And so it rises before us, the sole Purpose of all Creation, as splendid as eternal life and as inescapable as death."

Which is why, at the coordination meeting, he delivers the following preliminary report:

"Contents: The author of the pamphlet takes pleasure in deriding the aesthetic norms of socialist realism. In his view, the simple fact of Communism claiming a supreme goal makes it comparable to a standard monotheistic religion. The numerous Soviet authors targeted include Gorky and Lenin, about whom the author has the impertinence of making insolent remarks. The anti-Soviet character of this article is beyond doubt.

"Leads: The author has read our great contemporary Soviet writers. His lexical range is rich. His erudition is consummate. He appears well versed in biblical scripture. Among other rare occurrences, one notices the word 'Poland'. The abundant list of authors cited will be the object of further study (frequency, context).

"Actions considered: In Paris: intelligence gathering by our contacts associated with the journal *Esprit*. In the Soviet Union: targeted work with our informants in the large universities (Moscow, Leningrad, Kiev). Ascertain whether they remember any critical remarks they might have heard about socialist realism as a literary or artistic style. Ask them to be vigilant with regard to this subject in future, and to take it into account in their explorations."

The file answers to the administrative name of II-8-1959-Esprit-C. The first two numbers show the directorate responsible for the case. The "C" is a level of importance, on a scale ranging from A (absolute priority) to E (minor importance).

"C" is not much, really, without being of no consequence for all that. The author of the anonymous pamphlet is not a primary concern for the Competent Authority – his critique of the regime is veiled, operating by ricochet over academic literary works, rather than by frontal assault. However, there is the aggravating factor of his passing the manuscript to the West, and its publication (without previous authorisation) in a bourgeois journal. And that is not something that will be tolerated.

Ivanov implements his action plan. The French trail seems promising. We have sympathisers over there, at all levels. "Somebody knows!" as Colonel Vorontsov was wont to repeat. You just need to flush that someone out, and to work them skilfully.

Our contacts in the cultural mission in Paris rapidly come back with information about the obscure journal. Edited by Emmanuel Mounier until his death in 1950, then by Albert Béguin until 1957, *Esprit* has always been fascinated by the Leninist revolution ("a workers' and peasants' regime, progressive and spontaneous", Mounier wrote), even if Stalin's exploits occasionally caused dissension among the staff. Since the appointment of Domenach, a solid anti-Stalinist, the editorial line has been less clear.

There must be some way to approach Domenach and make him spill the beans. There's the Bald Smoker. There's the Seducer. Both those charlies have recently published articles in the journal. They are loyal agents of influence. We can ask them to lend a hand.

Ivanov takes all the necessary steps to this end. He passes on the information to whom it may concern.

While waiting for the anonymous author to get stung

(he doesn't stand a chance), there are the more pressing "B" files to be getting on with.

II-8-Zhivago-B. A delegation of Russian chemists, returning from a conference in Vienna, brought back several copies of *Doctor Zhivago* in their luggage. We detected this far too late. Now we will have to make sure that no copies of the forbidden book have escaped into the wild. Which means discreetly monitoring the comings and goings of all those people – but not actually going so far as to arrest them (that would be over-reacting). A serious discussion with each of them is called for. Not to mention giving a good ticking off to those who were in charge of the "security" of the trip.

II-8-Orwell-B. A university literature student and Komsomol member has been organising a reading group at his home, where under the pretext of improving their English, those pipsqueaks read George Orwell's *Nineteen Eighty-Four* aloud. It is now a matter of urgency to find out how that book found its way into our country. Infiltrate and dismantle the channel. Punish those responsible of such moral laxity with expulsion from the Komsomol and a good dose of community service work. It just so happens that there are several hundred bags of cement waiting to be unloaded at the Fokino cement factory.

Books, books, always more books!

Alongside all this work, Lieutenant Ivanov does some field training. He is sent to Smolensk, to an operations branch, where he observes the dismantling of a network of clandestine recordings, called "jazz on bones".

"So we'll never get rid of those 'bones' then?" Larissa asks, in disgust.

She once had the opportunity of handling one of these records: a friend, thinking she would like it, had given her Cab Calloway engraved on an X-ray plate. She enjoyed neither the music nor the malformation of the thorax you could see on the transparency, nor the process of buying the thing from a speculator's open coat flap.

Of course they're still around! The mania for jazz is a frightful thing. As soon as one business is dismantled, another one blooms in its place. D.I.Y. types are mad about it. To assemble the engraving contraptions, you just have to replace a record-player stylus with a harder needle, and pick up plates from radiology units. Nobody cares what you can see on them: a fractured tibia or lung cancer. The celluloid is an ideally soft material for tattooing those savage vibrations, those bestial romps.

In this case, the plates were filched from the paediatric unit of the Smolensk central hospital, and engraved with Miles Davis' "Birth of the Cool". In a numbered series, no less. The fine team was particularly proud of the sound-reproduction quality, and arrogant enough to put their copyright mark in the centre of the record.

Surveillance, stakeouts, arrests of students in the act of peddling the precious merchandise – confiscated and immediately destroyed – identification of the workshops, searches. The owner of the engraving turntable gets six years. His accomplice at the hospital, four. Expulsions from university for the young hawkers. For minor accomplices, community service work: hoeing a field of sugar beets at the "Red Proletarian" kolkhoz.

Out of curiosity, Ivanov once tried to listen to a Miles Davis record on bones. Unbearable! It sounded like a cat yowling in the middle of the night at −10°C.

Books and jazz fill his days. It is already July. The first results of the French investigation have come in. They are disappointing. The Bald Smoker is actually no longer being invited to the parties that Domenach goes to. As for the Seducer, his conversation with the secretary at the journal's offices was a total waste of time: no-one has any idea where the article came from.

It's a deadlock. For want of any clues, file II-8-1959-Esprit-C falls to the middle of the pile, and into neglect. Especially since an absolutely top priority case has turned up: II-8-1959-Sokolniki-A.

"A" as in: the Central Committee of the Party is involved. "A" as in: Shelepin, the great leader of the Competent Authority, has called his senior officers to a meeting.

Sokolniki is not a high-flying spy who has betrayed his homeland. Nor a revolutionary new cypher. Nor the code-name of a covert operation or a submarine.

Sokolniki is a park where the American National Exhibition has just opened, a gigantic whirlwind of cars, colour television sets, kitchen appliances, ready-to-wear apparel, potato crisps, popcorn, chewing gum... Opened in person by the biggest cheeses of all, the vice-president of the United States Richard Nixon and Nikita Khrushchev, the show is driving the entire population of Moscow bonkers. Seventy-five thousand visitors on opening day. Queues five hours long just to get a ticket – the forgers are having a field day. At night, intrepid fanatics dig tunnels under the perimeter fence to penetrate into Paradise. Others, once they get inside, find hiding places and refuse to leave.

"Whose idea was it to let the Americans come to Moscow with all their junk?" the qualified forces mutter. "It's bedlam! How are we supposed to control all this?"

Ivanov is worried: how can you be sure that the desire for abundance won't spread to vulnerable people?

"This is a test of our moral values," Captain Nikonovich declares. "The communist man, filled with the ideals of progress and universal humanism, must show himself to be indifferent to all this razmataz."

It must be said, however, that very few citizens appear to have the required faith. Most of them are drooling with envy and incredulity. It's a shambles. A counter-attack must be mounted at once. Hence II-8-1959-Sokolniki-A.

The entire eighth directorate is mobilised. Lieutenant Ivanov is charged with organising the Komsomol groups, those morally irreproachable young bloods who will bear the sword into the very stands of the enemy and heckle the hostesses about their capitalist lies and omissions.

The washing machine exhibit is forced to come face to face with its contradictions. The youths attack:

"You tell us you are liberating women from a chore, but only rich people can afford to own one of these contraptions. Meanwhile, the owner of the factory that manufactures them is lining his pockets."

Or else:

"Here in the Soviet Union, even though not everyone has a washing machine yet, soon we will catch up with America, and every family will get one, for free."

Faced with these tornadoes, the American representatives are disoriented. Ashamed, they avoid answering back. You can tell they aren't up to it. Lost, they smile at everyone around them with naive expressions. Ah! that American smile, displayed like the stars and stripes!

"Take it easy, guys," Captain Nikonovich appeases them. "We're not out to frighten the Yankees. Remember they are our guests."

Nevertheless, Ivanov observes that the tight-lipped crowd of ordinary Russians, gawking at the merchandise in a hypnotic trance, doesn't seem to set much store by our moral superiority.

At the Pepsi-Cola stand, it's just madness: there's no way to push through the crowd of people, who sometimes wait for hours for their free cup of the carbonated drink. Under the shock of this new taste, the weak spend all day getting a fix of Pepsi. Once they have swallowed their serving of ambrosia, they immediately go back to the end of the queue to wait for more. What is this devilry?

One particularly enterprising chap boasts he has already had ten drinks of it. He has kept the precious ten paper cups, handling them as if they were Fabergé eggs.

"Please follow me," Ivanov says as he collars him discreetly. "I've got a couple of things to say to you."

Citizens like this one, fascinated by everything that comes from the West, are the weak links in our system. They are on the slippery slope towards moral capitulation, forgetting their forebears who gave their lives during the civil war to overthrow tsarist oppression. They let their individualistic selfishness take over. "Consume, consume, consume!" they say, destroying all collective consciousness.

This is what Ivanov explains to the Pepsi guy, who does not appear to be convinced – you can see it in his eyes, which are looking for a way to escape.

"Khrushchev himself had a drink of Pepsi," he argues, when he is not withdrawn into prudent silence.

O.K., sure, but that's not the same thing! To start with, Nikita Sergeyevich is the First Secretary of the Party. You could say he's immune to Pepsi. And he didn't drink ten cups of it, did he? He was reasonable about it. It didn't go to his head and he didn't lose all his critical faculties as a result. Everyone was impressed when he put Nixon in his place at the kitchen appliance stand: "Really, how stupid can you be to use an electric contraption, when you can just pick up a lemon with your fingers and squeeze it into your tea!" That's what Khrushchev said, then he added "Per'aps you also need a machine to put the food into your mouth and shove it down your gullet?"

Embarrassed by this trucker's joke, Nixon forced himself to laugh.

The Pepsi guy is annoyed. He pretends to understand, but you can tell that all he's thinking about is how to get rid of the lieutenant and get back to his American bacchanalia. Behold the power of the Western flu virus!

In the absence of any directives, Ivanov cannot take him away or summon him later to continue his re-education. He does, however, make a note of his name: Vasily Lipkin.

"Right, Vasily, I've got you in my sights now. If we ever find any Pepsi cups on the black market, we'll know it's you. Go on, clear off now."

And what do you think Vasily did? He pretended to be interested in the cars for a bit, then went straight back to the Pepsi queue.

"Don't you want to come and try it?" says Captain Nikonovich, who already has two cups under his belt.

"No way," Ivanov says.

"It's not bad actually, but it's not good either," Nikonovich says. "Right, this'll be my last one. 'Know your enemies', as General Suvorov used to say."

There's no way not to know them here – they're everywhere, spread over an area of more than 41,000 square metres.

Ivanov goes to get his group of faithful Komsomols so they can sign the exhibition's visitors' book. Each one of them is bursting with the urge to show the upper hand, each one has prepared a riposte. Irina: "Thank you for the exhibition, but all your products are expensive and not very useful." Sergei: "American books are printed with low quality ink." Volodya: "Your medical system is unaffordable; our medical care is free."

When you leaf through the results, you can be proud of the home of socialism. On paper, the citizens seem to have their priorities right. "Your mask of cheerful consumerism cleverly hides your desire to exploit the proletariat," writes a certain Samsonov, an engineer at the Moskvich factory. Did he come up with this all on his own, or was he being monitored? Who's to know?

Ivanov is shocked at the contrast: the lucidity of the visitors' book is in stark opposition to the gawping attitude of thousands of visitors, who are in a state of absolute shock – all dilated pupils, high-pitched giggles, garrulous choppy exclamations, like hiccups:

"The fabric, look at the fabric, can you see it, the fabric? Can you see it? That skirt, I mean, take a look at the fabric on that skirt! Don't push in now, be nice, citizenochka, I was here first!"

Others, as if stunned by an anvil of happiness, wander

aimlessly about, their sandals raising puffs of summer evening dust.

At the Fialka café just across from the park, Ivanov takes a break and thinks about the difficulties of the fight waged by the fatherland of Communism against the American mastodon. Of course Khrushchev did promise to catch up with America, then to overtake it – the promise is inscribed in the five-year plan – but very few of our fellow citizens seem to cleave strongly enough to the virtue required to believe it.

The Soviet press, mobilised alongside the Competent Authority, understands what is at stake. What a pleasure it is to read an article in *Izvestia* about the American modern art presented at the exhibition. Jackson Pollock's *Cathedral* is described as a "childish scribble", and the insightful critic even sees it as a symptom of the "degenerescence of capitalism".

Here's hoping that's true, and that capitalism, rotten to the core, will end up bursting under its own weight when it falls down to the foot of the banana tree. Here's hoping.

In the meantime, while the press can plaster over the cracks and the Competent Authority can educate the people, the psychological damage is still considerable.

Long after Sokolniki, you still find entry tickets kept fondly at the bottom of drawers of unfulfillable dreams. Souvenir badges, Pepsi cups, Ford and Chrysler brochures, colour photographs of Silver Match lighters, chewing gum wrappers…

In 1972 during a search of a dissident painter's flat, the operatives find pages from an art book by an American publisher exhibited at Sokolniki, cut out with a piece of a razor blade cleverly hidden in a ring. When he hears about it, Ivanov feels slightly faint with shame. As if he were personally responsible for the proliferation of Western baubles in his fellow citizens' secret drawers.

III

At K-Prep, under the strict yet generous authority of Colonel Vorontsov, Ivanov used to love the handbooks, pocket-sized, hardbound, of around a hundred pages each, with plain grey or drab blue canvas covers. At the top on the right-hand side, the word "SECRET" was stamped in capital letters, and each copy of the booklet was numbered to allow regular checks that none had gone missing in action. It was forbidden to take them out of the school grounds. You could only consult them in the library, in a special reading room. Even copying out extracts was not allowed. But there was nothing to stop you learning passages off by heart, then hurrying to your notebook once you were out of the library to get them down in writing before your memory gave up – without, of course, shouting from the rooftops that you were doing this. That way you could study in secret during the evenings in the dormitory, to prepare for your exams.

With practice, Ivanov was able to ingest longer and longer passages, opening up new filing drawers in his brain. These days he still gets a thrill from mentally reciting certain passages, like the paragraph on informants, taken from the handbook *Political Intelligence on the Territory of the*

U.S.S.R.: "The recruitment of informants is achieved through both a gradual implication of the persons approached and a direct recruitment proposal. This can be secured by a written engagement regarding voluntary consent to confidential collaboration with the staff. The recruitment report will then show the alias chosen by the informant."

Informants – one of the lieutenant's strong points. Which is just as well, since a sustained increase in their numbers is one of the key performance indicators for promotion.

Ivanov handles around thirty of them. A time-consuming and delicate task. He is responsible for their training, the regular collection of pertinent information, and monitoring their psychological aptitude. A demotivated informant, who supplies unreliable or unusable information, can be a real time-waster, or even compromise the entire mission of working a target.

When Pinecone, a podgy and affable physicist, forgets to come to two consecutive meetings, the lieutenant senses that it is time to take him in hand again. He is accosted on leaving the office and they have a conversation – frankness is called for with the Competent Authority, just as it is with a doctor.

Why this exhausted look? Your shoes not polished? The grease stain on your tie? What about the Fatherland in all this? Why this radio silence?

His breath is normal and his hands aren't shaking – not an alcohol problem, then.

It turns out that everything can be explained by his complicated family situation. Pinecone was foolish enough to engage in a liaison with one of the interns at the Institute, who is now threatening to tell all to his wife. The fickle husband is trying to manage both the hare and the hound, and doesn't have the headspace to collect information anymore. He isn't going to parties, or to the Young Physicists' Club, he didn't even bother going to his own university class reunion. He's thoroughly lost inside his navel, is Pinecone.

"You should have told me," Ivanov scolds him. "You can't leave missions hanging. Of course you're allowed to have personal issues – who doesn't? – but if everyone did as you do, just imagine it, putting their paltry personal life before duty, then the whole structure of the State would be compromised."

With their oversized egos, elite physicists are easy prey for sirens from the West, just like all high-flying scientists. Pinecone is indispensable in tracking down and reporting the first symptoms of the disease. He needs to pull himself together, dammit!

But the lieutenant also knows how to reassure his informant. Just because he has strayed doesn't mean that from one day to the next he has lost his value. No-one would hold it against him if he spaced out his deliveries. It's understandable that they might need to make allowances.

To show how much the Competent Authority values him, Ivanov gives him two tickets to the ballet, "The Coast of Hope", by the Kirov company currently having a season in Moscow. An edifying performance about the professional life of workers at sea – the lieutenant checked. After a storm, a Soviet fisherman lands on an unknown shore. But it won't be a picnic. He is tortured by enemies of the Revolution, then finally saved by internationalist proletarians who show up in a mass demonstration.

The Kirov – there's nothing better. Pinecone must go with his wife. It will be the perfect opportunity to announce to her that, all going well, they will be offered a stay at a sanatorium in Crimea next summer. When you are a communist, a traditional, legally wedded wife is capital. Stability. Education of future generations. Balance. So, Pinecone, get stuck in again! Get stuck in with cement!

"I'm counting on you. Forgive me for being vulgar, but don't let yourself be led by your dick – you, a fighter for the proletarian cause. For my part, I'll ask a loyal student to calm the little intern down a bit, and douse the fire in her arse. What did you say her name was?"

It takes all of Ivanov's patience and enthusiasm to find the right words to say, to unravel inextricable situations, and sometimes, to cut to the quick. Break up definitively with an agent. Threaten. Punish. Model the human clay, in fact.

Going through his files, Ivanov feels like he's the daddy of a large family, with all the attendant responsibilities, joys and troubles.

The work is productive: he's lost count of all the crimes detected and enemies neutralised thanks to his devoted little ants.

Informants are your best resource in intellectual circles, where operatives always flounder.

Saying so in no way diminishes the merits of the Competent Authority.

How else would you infiltrate this aristocracy where everyone spends their days splitting hairs?

How can you be sure whether a piece of writing is anti-Soviet or not, unless someone reads it?

You can't be everywhere, hear everything, work it all out by yourself. Especially since some people write literary stuff, with interminable sentences. It's just inhuman.

Which is why, once the priority mission at Sokolniki is over, Ivanov returns to his darlings. With the journal *Esprit* still in his sights, he makes the following entry in the operation's file: "It would be useful to work with university circles in the widest sense of the term (professors, students, librarians) to track down any direct or veiled criticism of what is known as socialist realism. Who has expressed an unconventional opinion on the subject? Take note of any derision. Do not hesitate to start a conversation on the topic and to provoke responses skilfully. Scrupulously note the person's name, the date and any references quoted."

Monocle shows himself to be particularly interested in the mission – he loves provocation.

Monocle is a dandy, an architect by training, a specialist on Asia. He cultivates a wide circle of liberal-minded friends he loves to show off to by reciting forbidden poems by Mandelstam or Akhmatova. He has some success with women. He is called Monocle because he wears big round glasses. During his first encounter with the Competent Authority, in the twilight of a late September evening, one of the lenses of his glasses gleamed and became opaque: Monocle! He liked his secret identity straight away. He assumed it with delight.

Monocle did not get into denunciation out of loyalty to ideology. He has no faith in Communism's radiant future. Paradoxically, this makes him even more effective – he doesn't risk appearing awkward or insincere when he infiltrates real enemies of the Soviet people. No-one can pretend better than he can to be an embittered intellectual frustrated by the restrictions of censorship. You should see him lamenting the fate of Pasternak! Or expressing in crude terms how petit-bourgeois consumers are sick to the back teeth of empty shelves in the shops. He naturally enters into collusion with his targets. He catalyses their confessions, and archives everything in his memory. An excellent asset, cynical and manipulative, who takes pleasure in feeling and exerting his power.

Monocle in the first line, but also Aurora Borealis (a woman), Chichikov and Dickens, among other devoted little soldiers, are sent off fishing for information. Ivanov motivates his troops with shopping vouchers for the Voentorg department stores, reserved for officers. You can find quite a few scarce products there at affordable prices: in these last few months of 1959, Hungarian toothpaste is top of the bestseller list, along with Cuban bananas so green you have to hang them under your bed for a month before they ripen up and become edible.

Despite his informants' devotion to duty, the results are slow in coming. It seems socialist realism is not a hot topic. Nobody wants to study it. And even less to critique it. The educated elite accept it as you accept the cold in wintertime. Socialist realism is an imposed constraint and there's nothing you can do about it; that would be like hammering your fists on a mountainside hoping that it will move. Everyone just ignores it, or pretends to ignore it.

"These days it's more Picasso that the young people get excited about," Monocle reports.

Picasso, the name rings a bell. Ivanov knows that he is

a member of the French Communist Party, no doubt the most celebrated and least disciplined one ever – what bee got into his bonnet to make him criticise how we sorted out Hungary in 1956?

That same year, the first Picasso exhibition shook Moscow. Ivanov did not go (he's not really interested in the fine arts, even though he does like Ilya Repin's vast canvases). But he is aware of the shockwave it created. Just as at Sokolniki, there was a never-ending queue. And heated discussions. "What's the value of his 'Dove of Peace', if he didn't spend more than a minute drawing it?" "Any five-year-old can draw like Picasso!"

For Ivanov, when he has the time to think about it, those twisted proportions are just a bad joke. A case in point: the portrait of Stalin on the cover of *Lettres françaises*. What an impertinence! The great leader was given a chubby face and large effeminate eyes, he looked like nothing more than a kindly dolt. No majesty, no depth of thought in Picasso's Stalin. Not a good likeness either – and it wasn't for lack of photographs that the dauber could have used for inspiration.

In France, furious comrades flooded the journal and its editor, Louis Aragon, with enraged missives. They were quite right to be indignant. No, that was not Stalin's face! "The veneration, the love that I, like all the good people of France and the world, feel for the late great leader were strongly shocked by this graphic representation that in no way reflected the luminous character, intelligence and fraternity of Stalin!" wrote a lady from Montrouge, in a letter published alongside Aragon's *mea culpa*.

And now, in the very fatherland of Communism, that

self-same Picasso is turning heads. What is it that people see in him?

"He is the exact opposite of socialist realism," Monocle tries to explain, from the heights of his erudition.

"But what have you all got against socialist realism?" the lieutenant wonders. "At least you can see the labour, the sweat, the technical mastery of the artists, which cannot be said of Picasso and his blotches."

Monocle weighs up the Competent Authority with a cold contemptuous stare:

"Picasso has a kind of internal freedom. But I don't like everything he does," he adds cautiously. "Sometimes Comrade Picasso gets it wrong. Too much formalism distances him from the proletariat. He is condemned to be misunderstood by the masses."

"Exactly!" Ivanov exults. "You took the words right out of my mouth. I get the sense that Picasso, comrade though he may be, is looking down his nose at us with his art, when we are the ones who are at the front lines of world revolution. Picasso is not aligning himself with us on the level of historical reality."

Monocle keeps quiet. There's no point in talking aesthetics with this goon, who is about as sensitive to the fine arts as a washtub. He thinks about his school friend Andrei, and stifles a guffaw. He would go crazy, Andrei would, if he heard him saying that. "Picasso is not aligning himself with us" – language like reinforced concrete! Andrei, who somehow managed to visit the Picasso exhibition twice, and collects every last postcard he can find. Badly printed or torn, who cares, as long as it's Picasso!

Ivanov is immediately vigilant, like a bird of prey:

"What's there to laugh about?"

"Nothing. I was just thinking of an old friend. A Picasso-idolater."

That softhead is hoping to publish a book on Picasso, the first to be written in Russian. Good luck to him. Monocle would be extremely surprised if he managed to pull it off – when you know how thin-skinned and lily-livered editors can be about that self-same "level of historical reality".

"Let's get back to socialist realism," Ivanov suggests. "Keep your eyes open, and your ears. You are my best asset."

There's no need for concert tickets or Voentorg passes to motivate Monocle. That would almost be insulting. Flattery, on the other hand, coming from the heart and with a whiff of good old virile complicity, that's what gets him going.

IV

At the end of the autumn of 1959, the Competent Authority learns of the publication in Paris, in the Polish dissident journal *Kultura*, of a new short story by the same anonymous writer. Well, anonymous is not quite accurate anymore, since the man now has a pseudonym, Abram Tertz.

Ivanov has a go at reading this one too – only this time it's easy, it's printed in Russian. Entitled "The Trial Begins", it is a story about prosecutors and adultery. Scenes of female nudity blossom from the second chapter onwards. The word "Trotskyism" appears on several pages – never a good sign. Why rub salt into the wounds? It all ends up in the Gulag, in Kolyma. There's not a shred of doubt, this disgusting tale could never have been published in the Soviet Union.

That name, Abram Tertz, is unknown to the Competent Authority. Just to set his mind at rest, Ivanov checks the telephone books for Moscow, Leningrad, Kiev, Kazan… Sometimes crackpots do actually sign anti-Soviet tracts with their own name.

This is not the case with Abram Tertz.

They talk about it at the canteen, over their bowls of cabbage soup.

"You need to try anagrams," Kulakov suggests. "Arty types are such narcissists, it's impossible for them not to sign their work. It's like a compulsion. Tertz could be the name of one of his grandfathers. Or it's the initials, A and T, which he borrowed from his real name."

Shmakov chortles. "What I see, actually, and you'll forgive me for calling a spade a spade, what I see is that he is Jewish."

Everyone agrees. Abram Tertz – you can't get more Jewish than that.

Shmakov, Kulakov and Ivanov being one hundred per cent Russian themselves.

"I've noticed a thing," Shmakov says. "The speculators, the ones loitering around on the Sophia Embankment, well, I've noticed that they're all Jewish too, mostly."

"Especially the richest ones," Kulakov adds. "They're the most cunning ones."

Ivanov then remembers a detail.

"At the beginning of 'The Trial Begins', the character of the prosecutor talks about –" he instinctively lowers his voice – "… about Trotsky. And he mentions that Trotsky is Jewish."

Shmakov is appalled.

"Trotsky wasn't Jewish! That's anti-Soviet propaganda!"

Suddenly, like a cold rain shower, they realise they've talked just a little too much about Trotsky, so they hurry up and finish their soup, stuffing it into their bellies with a serving of buckwheat kasha, nicely cooked with onions. A slice of black bread, and away they go.

The notion of an anagram is a good one. Ivanov spends

some time looking through the phone books for a Marbre Ztat, or a Tabar Mertz. No results. As for A.T., well there are millions of them. And Jews? Don't even mention it!

Meanwhile, and within only a few months, "The Trial Begins" is translated into a dozen languages. The Western literary journals are crazy about it, and generally publish it alongside *On Socialist Realism*, with a preface describing the risks that Abram Tertz is taking by sending his work to the West. Pasternak never fails to get a mention. "A new Pasternak," they cry. "A man who has braved the repression of the Soviet regime."

A new Pasternak – that's all we need!

Ivanov has not read *Doctor Zhivago*. What's the point? He already knows what he would find there – he skimmed the summary in the confidential memorandum that was circulated to all staff. He does not like literature filled with doom and gloom and historical hysteria. Where are the positive heroes? The victories? What is the moral of the story?

It's obvious you can't publish *Doctor Zhivago* in the Soviet Union. But does that mean Pasternak had to go and send his manuscript to an Italian editor? Feltrinelli, communist though he may be, could sense a good deal coming his way, and didn't think twice about accepting it.

Picasso, Feltrinelli: who needs enemies when your friends show such moral laxity?

And then those bourgeois reactionaries went and awarded him the Nobel Prize. What a dire month October 1958 turned out to be.

Boris Polevoy, the eminent member of the Union of Soviet Writers and twice winner of the Stalin Prize, was infuriated: Pasternak is a Judas of the highest degree of perfidy, a "literary Vlasov", he even said.

Captain Nikonovich thinks the comparison is a bit far-fetched. Contrary to General Vlasov, Pasternak did not surrender to the Germans besieging Leningrad.

Out of curiosity, the captain takes the trouble of leafing through a copy of the cursed novel, printed in Holland and confiscated at the border – those mischievous imperialist propaganda-spreaders were distributing free copies to Soviet tourists at the Brussels Universal International Exhibition.

Five hundred pages! Such difficult language! So many characters! He goes straight to the epilogue. And even that is interminable. Then at the very end, there are those twenty-five poems. Quite a few Christian references. Lots of waiting and snow. Nikonovich feels as if he's out in the countryside, like when you open the front door and stand on the porch doing nothing, just breathing in the silence of twilight. Strange.

Nikonovich tucks the book away in one of his desk drawers under his copy of the Criminal Code. Maybe he'll get back to it.

In the meantime, not a day goes by without them discussing Pasternak.

We must avoid making him a martyr, is the assessment in high places.

Shmakov is furious.

"We should have neutralised Pasternak once and for all. Back in the good old days… The doughty Cheka… the N.K.V.D. … I don't understand why we are tolerating this."

What a thick brute he is!

"You need to be tactically clever," Pakhmonov says. "You can't go at him with a meat axe when international opinion is watching our every move."

"I don't see why not," Shmakov says.

Pakhmonov reassures him by saying Pasternak could be arrested at a moment's notice. You'd just have to snap your fingers. He is convinced that they've thought about it, up there. But you have to be more cunning than that. Our enemies would only be too delighted if we committed such an error – it even makes you wonder if they aren't actually pushing us in that direction. They would immediately use it to paint a vile picture of us, and we would lose much of our support in the West. Foreign media attention has created an invisible protective dome around Pasternak.

Shmakov shrugs, as if to say that all it would take is one good blow from a hammer and bang! there goes your dome!

Pakhmonov is forced to lose his temper.

"The orders are clear, Comrade Shmakov!"

Then, remembering that authority will never replace pedagogy, he explains it all again for the umpteenth time.

So, what is the ultimate goal? Worldwide proletarian revolution. Exactly. That means everywhere. Including in France, in Italy, on the moon, in Timbuctoo, everywhere. And the French and Italian communist parties are actually doing quite well, they have no trouble recruiting new members, you can count on them. You wouldn't want that momentum to seize up, now, would you? If we go too hard on Pasternak – who is insignificant on a planetary scale – we risk holding back our French and Italian comrades. Which would delay worldwide revolution.

"It's in our best interests to show ourselves to be human," Captain Nikonovich translates.

But let's not get carried away either.

We didn't cover Pasternak in kisses: no, he was expelled from the Writers' Union. Then the press was set to work on him, pages full of it. Indignant letters to the paper drumming on Pasternak's back. They were published, read at meetings, pinned up in schools, factories, canteens and offices. The hail broke the windows. The gusts of icy wind chilled your bones.

"Workers are scandalised by Pasternak's perfidious behaviour. He has not taken our Soviet reality into account, nor the opinions of his fellow writers who drew attention to his erroneous views. He has slandered our working class, collective farmers and intelligentsia. He is a traitor who has sold himself to the capitalists. He should be judged as an enemy." An ordinary missive, among hundreds of others of the same calibre. Signed by Comrade Rodionov, a grinding machine operator at the Likhachev automobile factory.

Pasternak finally bowed under pressure. He refused the Nobel Prize.

"We didn't even strip him of his Soviet citizenship," Shmakov still complains.

It's true, though. We could have torn up his passport. Even Mikhalkov talked about it. There's no greater light in the darkness than Sergei Mikhalkov: he wrote the lyrics to the Soviet national anthem. You can trust Mikhalkov. We could have booted Pasternak all the way to his dreamland in the West. And good riddance too! But instead, we keep him here at home, where he continues to blight our utopia.

The voice of the people rises from Shmakov's loins.

At the back of the second floor, in the corridor separating the seventh and eighth directorates, there is now a whole filing cupboard devoted to Pasternak. A dozen people are forever foraging there, day and night.

"Treat Pasternak's Nobel Prize as an opportunity to make improvements at all levels," Colonel Volkov urges them.

And improvements are made, indeed: shadowing the visitors at his dacha at Peredelkino, especially foreigners, allows you to understand how the network of ideological conspiracies is structured.

Each and every inward or outward letter goes through a decontamination chamber. Pasternak's handwriting is decrypted, with its pretentious pen strokes – as if he were painting every letter. You take a note of all the names, and often intercept the correspondents – there's no question of him swaggering around with them in such barbarous anti-Sovietism.

A good call, as it turns out: while pretending to turn down the Nobel Prize, Pasternak is sending love letters to his foreign publishers. He congratulates them, cajoles them, blesses them. And refuses to allow his royalties to be administered by the Soviet government.

Shmakov: "I told you he was a piece of work!"

Western press: "Despite terrible pressure, Pasternak is not surrendering! Pasternak's cry is shaking up the Party and its apparatchiks."

They don't miss a trick, those bourgeois journos. They exaggerate everything, take their fantasies to be reality, but they never let up. Luckily their memory is as short as a sparrow's, and they quickly forget what they wrote the previous day. One emotion replaces another. All you have to do is wait.

Compiling, translating and summarising the fallout in the foreign press is terribly time-consuming. By dint of retyping miles of newspaper columns from French, English, Italian, Swedish etc., the enemy is familiar to the Competent Authority, literally to the very tips of its fingers, which are covered in callouses.

All that work. All that science.

But then at last the operations branch reports some good news: the writer is too old. He is ill. He is expected to croak any day now. Lung cancer. One year max.

Everyone is relieved. That'll get rid of one thorn in our side!

Pasternak is ill. Pasternak is dying.

Pasternak is dead.

At the funeral, on June 2, 1960, anyone in Moscow with the soul of a dissenter rushes to Peredelkino, preceded by the operations branch observing all this in-crowd, taking pictures, discreetly interrogating people to find out their names.

Captain Nikonovich has brought along a movie camera. He films people up close so he can identify them later. That's quite a challenge: he only has twenty minutes of film. So he focuses on the front door of the house and those who approach it. You'll likely find the most dangerous elements in the immediate proximity of the dead body.

A crackpot starts reciting a poem by Pasternak. It's old Balashov, well known to the Competent Authority – code name "Reader". A mediocre asset when it comes to reporting delicate information. But what charisma when he starts croaking out verse! Nikonovich can't help filming him, when that's really not the point.

Monocle is there too, at the epicentre of events. He's donned a black arm band over an American-style checked shirt.

Ivanov observes him from a distance. Then he loses sight of him in the huge crowd. It's madness!

His intuition tells him Abram Tertz is somewhere here too.

He is here in the crowd, enjoying his anonymity, mocking them.

Suddenly you can hear a piano. It's a pro playing, you can be sure of it. Chopin escapes from the wide-open house in endless outbursts.

"Who's the ivory tickler?" Shmakov says.

Nikonovich, a bit of a music lover, has already found out.

"Sviatoslav Richter."

"The music is really beautiful, though, isn't it?" Shmakov gushes.

Nikonovich talks to Major Kutilo, Richter's monitor. They're being sent on tour to the U.S.A. this autumn. It will be quite the event: Chicago, Carnegie Hall, and so on. And that numskull of a pianist doesn't even want to go, he's afraid of flying. They're all but begging him. It's just unfathomable.

The mystery of Sviatoslav Richter…

People are arriving from every direction, huddling together, carrying bouquets. They're all glad to see that they're not alone.

There's something like joyful connivance in the air, despite the poet's death.

Soon all Nikonovich can see is the backs of people's heads. He stops his movie camera and climbs up a tree to take his photographs from a better angle.

Perfect strangers are striking up conversations:

"Hi. I saw a handwritten announcement stuck on a wall in a train station in Moscow: 'Boris Pasternak, one of our greatest contemporary poets, has just passed away. The civil ceremony will take place today at 3 p.m. Peredelkino.'"

"Yes, that's here."

"How many do you think there are of us?"

"A thousand? Twelve hundred?"

"I'd say more like four thousand!"

Why not ten thousand while you're at it, Ivanov thinks. Eight hundred, max.

"That's huge!"

"The train was packed."

Ivanov realises that the Competent Authority will never ever be able to identify them all!

Even if we massively recruit more interns. Especially since we're in the middle of staff cutbacks.

And there's hardly enough space in the offices anyway. What with all that paperwork we're supposed to keep.

Later on, perched up in a tree above the head of an English journalist who is shooting questions at everyone, Lieutenant Ivanov pulls himself together. Let us not get discouraged. He counts and counts again, gets muddled, starts over. The ocean of heads is constantly moving.

Monocle spots his mate Andrei in the crowd. He's with Yuli, a translator, a charming Bohemian type. No wonder they're in the first rows, those two freaks. Andrei used to correspond with Pasternak, if Monocle remembers rightly, and he's quite proud of it too, even if he doesn't blow his trumpet about it. Yuli writes poetry as well. He knows hundreds of lines of Pasternak's verse. Monocle knows quite a few himself. Just last summer, in the middle of the *Zhivago* scandal, he was able to attract a fair bit of feminine attention, swaggering and crooning as he recited "My Sister – Life".

Here goes, they're bringing the coffin out. Enthusiasts are fervently taking turns carrying it.

A motorbus chartered by the Writers' Union is offering its services to take the body to the cemetery, quick smart, to get it all over and done with, without all this circus in front of the foreign press. The family protests. Pasternak is carried by hand, above the crowd, along the dusty path.

"The coffin remains open," an astonished Swedish journalist exclaims into his microphone. "It's the Russian tradition. And there are so many flowers!"

The procession crosses a field. Monocle remembers to tuck the bottoms of his trouser legs into his socks, so they don't get dirty.

At the cemetery, the crowd becomes compact, protective.

A speech, not a very long one. A poem. Then the heavy earth begins to fall.

The throng disperses rapidly – finally some good news for the Competent Authority.

But that doesn't mean the day is over. A few exalted young people stay on, taking turns to recite poems in the fading light. One guy has lit a candle, using it to read aloud the scribbles in his notebook in a monotone voice, while rocking back and forth. Lovers cast verses at each other. A guitar ripples in the distance.

Ivanov keeps an eye on this pack of loonies while waiting for the order to round them all up – which never comes.

"Let's go," Nikonovich ends up saying. "Let's terminate the operation and go home to bed."

In the van taking them back to the capital, Ivanov mulls over the report he will have to write the following day. Alongside the operational elements, and the chronology of the facts, he intends to launch into an assessment-outlook analysis.

"Given the large number of young people seen at the funeral, it would be judicious for the Writers' Union and the Ministry of Culture to prioritise their educational work with students and circles of artistic youth. This will allow us to combat the unhealthy humours and fallacious images held by some young people (a minority, thankfully) regarding Pasternak, whom they portray as a great artist, misunderstood in his time."

"What if Abram Tertz was… Pasternak?" Lieutenant-Colonel Pakhmonov asks during a staff meeting.

Pakhmonov has just read an Agatha Christie mystery (in English, from a book confiscated during a search), where the culprit was the narrator, which was why no-one had suspected him.

The cunning hypothesis is discussed.

Abram Tertz is Jewish, like Pasternak. He is erudite. He has a distinct sympathy towards Poland, like Pasternak.

In that regard, Pakhmonov reminds the meeting that the first extracts of *Doctor Zhivago* were published in 1957, in Warsaw, in the quarterly journal *Opinie*, which earned our Polish comrades a serious dressing-down.

With all due respect to his superior officer, Lieutenant Ivanov has a few reservations.

While the Polish coincidence is disturbing, nevertheless one must remember that there is Poland and Poland. Abram Tertz was published by an émigré dissident journal in Paris. Nothing like Pasternak, who benefitted from the appalling laxity of a "fraternal" country.

And it's also worth noting that Abram Tertz does not appear to have any particular connection with Italy, which was Pasternak's preferred route to publication.

The biggest difference is this one: Abram Tertz is remaining resolutely anonymous. Pasternak paraded in broad daylight, or might as well have done, whereas Abram Tertz is hiding like a tapeworm.

Pasternak was too self-assured, really.

Too famous, as well. And too old. As if he were possessed by a universal disgruntlement.

In other words, there's no good reason why Pasternak would have taken a pen name.

"What does the semantic analysis of his writing show?" Pakhmonov says.

The findings are incontrovertible: Abram Tertz is nothing like Pasternak. The anonymous writer displays "a tendency towards pamphleteering and irony", uses vocabulary "taken from daily Soviet life, which he appears constantly to be deriding", and has absolutely no interest in landscapes or nature.

Time passes. Ivanov is summoned to Colonel Volkov's office.

"Sit down, Evgeny. Your report on Pasternak's funeral has been appreciated in high places. Investigator Pakhmonov is full of praise for your analytical skills. Your network of informants is expanding and strengthening. Keep it up, young man. It's through combining field analysis and long-term strategic thinking that we will build up tomorrow's Competent Authority."

All of this without the slightest smile.

Ivanov feels like he's on Sputnik. Along with these kind words, he gets five days of extra leave and a pass – a yellow card, with his name handwritten onto it. Valid for a whole day, this little rectangle gives him access to the elite shops reserved for superior officers.

Which just goes to show he was right to raise his head over the parapet.

"Don't get too carried away with yourself," Nikonovich advises. "Of course having an overall view is a good thing, but only as long as your superiors feel validated."

That's an art in itself.

Good fortune multiplies as Ivanov finds out that his mother, Tamara Stepanovna Ivanova, who until now lived in a room of eight square metres in a communal apartment, has been allocated an individual apartment all to herself in a new building.

Her new life is in Cheryomushki, a residential area to the southwest of Moscow, a long way from the centre. On the top floor of a four-storey building.

All of it for her alone! Twenty-seven square metres all to herself! A kitchen (6 m^2), a bath and toilet nook (3 m^2) – all to herself! A 2.55 m stud height. Central heating. No lift. But the stairway is wide (not like the building across the street), and the steps are not too high to climb up comfortably.

Tamara has been very lucky. No-one can quite figure out how this apartment fell into her lap. Is it because of her feats of arms (she has a medal from the Great Patriotic War), or some scheming by her first husband, a former diplomat? Having a son in the Competent Authority can't do her any harm either, although no-one knows how high up he is.

Ivanov likes to think it is simply socialist providence at work.

Mama registered on the waiting lists as soon as they opened. She ticked "no preference" for the choice of neighbourhood. She waited five years. And the postman rang her doorbell!

Without her having to pay a kopek.

Not like in those reactionary countries where only the very rich have housing.

While anonymous Abram Tertz is being translated into a dozen languages and his calumny spreads throughout the world, Lieutenant Ivanov helps his old mother move into a brand-new apartment, which she got for free.

Adieu, thirty years of communal living! Adieu, Klavdia Petrovna, the madwoman who kept track of when Tamara went to the bathroom and made sure the water was cut off. Adieu, toilets black with mould where you had to bring your own toilet seat, then note on a piece of paper stuck to the door exactly how long you spent there so you could contribute fairly to the electricity cost of a meagre 25-watt bulb.

In her new apartment, there is no bulb and no electricity

in the toilet. Light comes in through a little window in the wall connecting it to the kitchen. You turn the light on in the kitchen, you go and do your business, then you go back and turn off the light. The energy savings are obvious. And the gloom doesn't encourage you to stay sitting for hours on the pot.

In the new apartment, she will have a wardrobe, instead of stashing her things under her bed.

Speaking of wardrobes, of course to begin with, she will not have a fridge. She'll manage. From October onwards it will be cold enough to put food in the little cupboard built in under the kitchen window – so practical! A panel only half a brick thick separates the inside from the outside: when it gets very cold, the food stored there can even freeze.

This magic cupboard does not stop her signing up to the waiting list for a fridge, even though it will not be altogether free. With his vouchers for Voentorg, her son is in a good position to get one after a shorter waiting period. The family spends a lot of time discussing the best strategy. Spend the coupons now and get it sooner, or wait for socialist providence and save the vouchers?

The shelving unit for the living room has been reserved since late last spring. On that front, things are looking promising. The assistant salesgirl, sensitive to an intellectual's charms (Ivanov wears glasses), promised that he would be among the first people to get one as soon as there was a delivery of "decent wood". Slight concern: no-one can be entirely sure which model will be delivered. A "shelving unit" is already a good thing. With a little luck (no harm in dreaming) it might even be a whole wall of shelves, with sliding glass doors. Very practical for books and porcelain ornaments. In the worst-case scenario (if the dimensions really don't fit), he'll resell the unit within an hour to one of the nobodies hanging around the shop, and probably make a small profit on the deal.

She'd like everything to be brand new, Tamara would. It's time she was reborn from her ashes. She gives the old moth-eaten carpet away to friends. The ancestral table, with its enormous ink stain soaked deep into the wood, goes to the dump. Ivanov takes charge of lugging all her old stuff there, and after one last nostalgic look at that table where he worked so hard on his homework as a boy, grabs a brick and crash! splinters the mahogany. Smash! smash! Away with the old, in with the new! New life, new things, new prosperity.

The only regret is that the trapdoor of the rubbish chute in the kitchen doesn't open properly.

Tamara's building is one of the first to be constructed at Cheryomushki as a remedy for the enormous housing shortage. The builders and architects were in a hurry. So with the rubbish chutes, in their urgency, they didn't think to measure the dimensions of the trapdoor properly. It gets stuck halfway open.

Abram Tertz, instead of making bad jokes, could have gently mocked this particularity of the rubbish chutes, the result of the carelessness that is a gangrene on our best intentions. He would have been applauded – constructive criticism is always welcome. He would have been published in *Krokodil*, the very hilarious satirical weekly. Print run: 1,400,000 copies.

That week Tamara had a good laugh when she saw the

following cartoon: inside a building that has just been constructed, the stairway is placed such that there is no access to the second floor. A bureaucrat from the Ministry of Housing raises a finger and proclaims in a speech bubble: "Let's not get distracted by these details, the apartment delivery is accomplished!"

"You see, Evgeny, that's exactly what happened with the rubbish chute."

And then to hear that you can't criticise anything in the land of the Soviets. It's just the opposite! Those who refuse to see the truth have such flagrant bad faith.

"Don't throw away your old issues of *Krokodil*, Mama," Ivanov replies as he examines the bubbles under the wallpaper in the hallway. "We'll need them to redo the walls."

Krokodil's smooth paper is better quality than *Pravda*'s. Impregnated with glue, it will be perfect for the base layer. It's what you use instead of plaster and primer, which you can't get hold of anywhere.

"My walls are fine, really."

Tamara has no desire to get carried away with renovations.

But it would be such a shame not to do it: in Leningrad, there's just been a delivery of Polish wallpaper at the local branch of Voentorg. The father of a friend could get hold of some.

Such opportunities do not present themselves every day.

Polish means fresh bright colours. Even though you have no idea what shades are available, the wallpaper won't be yellowish or faded lavender, as if it had been left to die in stagnant water.

The patterns will be a little more sophisticated than

the baskets of flowers and drooping garlands that everyone else has. Something surprising and different.

Polish means it won't decompose when you generously brush it with glue or have to tug at it as you are putting it up.

The time to decide is now!

Right, let's do it!

It will be magnificent!

Saturday fortnight, since he's not on call, Ivanov comes over with his mates Shurik and Lyonya. Each of them has two arms. Look how easily the task is dispatched! Splosh! Swish! The walls are covered with *Krokodil*, which has to be left to dry for a while. Shurik gets out a bottle.

"Not for me," Ivanov says categorically.

Alcohol, he is convinced, is a poison that destroys your moral compass. Anyone who drinks is a weak link compromising the entire nation's efforts.

It's because of alcohol that the rubbish chute doesn't open properly. Drinkers are unwitting saboteurs. And their weakness makes them vulnerable to anti-Soviet propaganda, if not to the siren calls of foreign intelligence agencies.

"On a Saturday?" Shurik is surprised. "How can you stay dry on a Saturday…?"

"Leave him alone," Lyonya says. "He's right."

Which doesn't stop Lyonya from pouring himself a glass. Then another one.

"To the conquest of the cosmos!" Shurik exclaims.

"To our fighter planes!"

"To our ground-based air defences!"

They're all thinking about the same thing: that U-2 spy

plane that was gunned down from the skies over their country.

Which is all the proof you need (if you ever needed any!) that the henchmen of capitalism are envious of the Soviet Union and trying to steal our secrets.

Which is also all the proof you need that we are not choirboys and we won't take it lying down!

We're not mincing our punches!

Their cutting-edge technology – boom!

And their pilot, Gary Powers, picked up safe and sound, with all his ultra-sophisticated equipment, his films, his flight plans, his targets.

And those U.S.A., spying on us behind our backs all this time, when last year, at Sokolniki, with the best will in the world, we organised a huge exhibition in their honour. Treachery, hypocrisy, fake smiles, smoke and mirrors!

Powers, the spy, was judged and sentenced to ten years in prison.

And when we catch Abram Tertz, he'll get a prison sentence too – Article 58-10 of the Criminal Code is there for that purpose. "Propaganda with the aim of weakening the power of the Soviet Union." The absolute minimum is six months. What the maximum might be is not entirely clear. Several years, no doubt. Publishing abroad is an aggravating circumstance.

It won't be ten years.

But it's hard to see it being less than five.

During the Ogre's reign, you would not have asked so many questions, you would have just gone bang! bang! as Shmakov would put it.

So, five years? That's rather lenient actually.

While he's mulling this over, Tamara cries, "Come and look at the building across the street!"

Over there, suspended through the open window of the third floor by two ropes on each side, a long black box is starting to move down.

"What are they up to?"

Everyone looks more carefully – it's a coffin!

On the ground, a city council car is waiting for the precious load. You can see them directing operations: let go of more rope on the right! Watch the balcony! Gently now!

The deceased has reached the height of the second floor. The ropes are taut. The box is swaying gently. Curious onlookers are gathering.

They finally understand the whys and wherefores of this manoeuvre: the front door and stairwell are too narrow. Once the coffin is out of the doorway, there's nowhere to turn. A board would manage it, but not a box. The window was the only remaining option. The comrade must have snuffed it at home. God knows how long they must have kept him there before attempting the evacuation down the front of the building.

Lyonya is deeply moved.

"May the earth be like a feather on you, my friend! What a shame to die in a new apartment."

He drains his glass.

The spectacle makes Tamara proud of her own stairway. Given the choice, she'd rather have a rubbish chute that doesn't open than a narrow staircase where you can't get a coffin through, let alone a fridge.

But she does wonder whether this isn't a bad omen. Ivanov gets annoyed.

"Oh come on, Mama, leave your peasant superstitions behind in the mire of petit-bourgeois prejudices!"

Upon which, taking the mystical presence of the flying stiff as a pretext, Shurik and Lyonya finish the bottle.

The rest of the day is less efficient, to be sure. No-one is actually sozzled, but no-one is seeing straight either. Except Ivanov. Ah, these flagging troops! How are we supposed to defeat the U.S.A.?

"You are judging us rather severely," Shurik says, but without taking serious offence. "Sure, we like to wet our whistle, but at least we aren't slaves to Polish wallpaper, like you are."

He marks a point.

The lieutenant does have the feeling that his recent preoccupations with furniture, the rubbish chute and the fridge might look like a headlong race towards material well-being, in direct contradiction with the new man that the Party is forging. A simple man, content with very little.

"It's for my mother!" he tries to justify himself. "Our elders deserve a few luxuries, don't they? Think of their sacrifices during the war!"

But his conscience is nagging him.

Which is why, once the work is finished, he gives the offcuts to his mates, instead of taking them home to do up his own hallway.

Larissa does not complain, far from it.

"We aren't tsars, we can wait for Soviet wallpaper, just like everyone else."

How proud he is right now to have a wife like Larissa!

They sip their cabbage soup and go into raptures about

their recent run of good luck: Tamara Stepanovna's apartment, the congratulations from Colonel Volkov, Larissa's new position at a school just down the road from their home.

When the stars align like that, it's a sign.

A nudge for them to get into bed and make babies.

They think about it while Larissa clears the table, washes and dries the dishes, then puts them away in the sideboard.

Then they turn off the light and go to it.

Even though they now have their own apartment, they make as little noise as possible – no unseemly squeals, no embarrassing moans. We're not animals! They got into the habit of discretion in the first years of their relationship, when their intimacy was wrought behind a folding screen in a communal apartment, at Larissa's parents' place.

Now, there's a man and a woman with perfect control of their instincts!

The box spring also keeps its trap shut.

When they're finished, to mask their embarrassment and forget what just happened, they talk about international politics.

"The Belgian Congo has struggled out from under the imperialist boot," Larissa observes.

A pause.

"He had it coming to him, the King of Belgium!"

Then Ivanov speaks up.

"Patrice Lumumba is a hero!"

Larissa is clear-sighted in spite of her fatigue.

"Of course there's still Katanga and that capitalist puppet Moïse Tshombe, who sold himself to the exploiters."

"He looks like a cannibal!" Ivanov jokes.

He lights up a Friend cigarette, and plays in the dark with the rattling matchbox.

Apart from Katanga, they easily agree that, with the independence of French Equatorial Africa, colonialist exploitation is in a bad way.

"Ghana is also free from the English yoke!"

"Africa is a house of cards!"

V

Monocle gets an unpleasant surprise. His friend Andrei's brochure about Picasso is being published by the very serious Znanie publishing house. It's not really a book – only eighty pages long – and it's just a paperback. Andrei is the co-author with Igor Golomstok, an art critic Monocle has met several times and who has always been impermeable to his charms – almost as if he could smell a rat.

The print run is substantial (100,000 copies) without being a tidal wave. In this country, anything printed at fewer than 300,000 copies is hard to find in the bookshops.

In the intellectual circles in which Monocle moves, the book creates a small sensation: perhaps it's a sign of the regime warming up.

The blurb on the back cover tries to square the circle, to show that modernity is not incompatible with Soviet orthodoxy: "The authors endeavour to explain the complexity and contradictions of Picasso's oeuvre, which defends a progressive political viewpoint, even though he expresses it through artistic means whose formalism is foreign to us."

Each word here is worth its weight in sweat.

You can just imagine the back and forth between the

editors at Znanie and the censors to get this tissue of compromises approved.

You can also sense a kind of vulnerability here. It wouldn't have taken much at all for the project to be torpedoed altogether.

Better late than never, Monocle thinks.

While sounding off to anyone who will listen that the great artist's blue period is better than his rose period (just to show he knows what he's talking about, and has done for quite some time now) he takes up his pen to write a strongly worded letter to the directors of Znanie.

"Picasso is not an artist, he's a charlatan! At the very moment when the fight for our promising ideals is particularly tense, notably in Africa, our young critics are glorifying decadent bourgeois art."

And he signs it with a made-up name: "Boris Stepanov, metalworker."

The voice of the proletariat is the trumpet of Jericho.

Monocle is not alone. Other readers are genuinely indignant.

Each of these letters is like a pin dipped in curare. If there are too many of them, heads will roll, obviously.

After a dozen or so letters received, Znanie is in a bind. The necessary measures must be taken. Better safe than sorry. A few days after its publication, the first book ever to be written in Russian about Picasso is no longer distributed in Moscow, and never even makes it to Leningrad. The entire run will moulder in an annexe at the printers. Then it will be pulped.

Andrei shrugs. "Well at least the book exists."

"You can be proud of it!" Monocle raves. "Your Picasso

63

is now a rarity sought after by bibliophiles. Just off the Arbat, I heard it was going for three roubles a copy."

"Old roubles or new roubles?" Andrei can't help asking.

It's just that since the beginning of the year, a currency reform has poked its nose into everyone's wallets. Everything has been divided by ten, prices and salaries.

"New, of course!"

That's a tidy added value for a brochure whose official price is nineteen kopecks.

"If you've got any spare author copies, now is the time to palm them off, you lucky bastard."

Hopeless businessman that he is, Andrei is not tempted.

He's having enough trouble getting used to the new banknotes – they're so small! They look like lolly wrappers.

Lenin is still there on the large denominations. Andrei notices that, in the bas-relief, he has struck a profile pose that accentuates his prominent jawline.

"A fossil, Lenin is!" Monocle exclaims. "A fossil who doesn't even dare look his citizens in the eye!"

The provocation draws no blood. Andrei shrugs again.

You'd think he was too preoccupied by the practical consequences of the reform.

He has until April 1 to change his money, but everyone knows (how, is anyone's guess) that you'd better hurry up. Starting on January 2, queues of several hours form in front of the savings banks.

People wait, get annoyed.

In the middle of winter, by temperatures of $-10\,°C$.

Blessed are those who haven't put any cash aside!

That's the case of Lieutenant Ivanov, who finished 1960 by blowing all his savings on a new sideboard for his mother.

Solid, light-coloured timber, made in Hungary, with two glass shelves above and three storage compartments below, one of which can be locked (the key was misplaced, they'll have to force the lock). Height 1.51 m, width 1 m, depth 45 cm. Its motto: "Modern furniture must have simple lines." Available on pre-registration for 350 new roubles and a waiting time estimated at twelve months, you can get it sooner as long as you know Zina, the manager of procurement at the furniture department of the foreign trade store, Vneshtorg.

Ivanov hopes to be able to land a deal for a carpet (130 roubles) from the same supplier, which will be perfect to hang on one of the walls as decoration and to reduce the neighbours' noise – his mother complains a lot about the thin partitions. In exchange for a tip, Zina agrees to put one aside. It will definitely be for Ivanov – unless another priority buyer with a superior rank shows up first.

It's not easy to take care of these purchases during working hours. Especially at the moment, with all the pressure he's under! The transition to new roubles is a total balls-up that has mobilised everyone.

The ingenuity of the swindlers knows no bounds, verging almost on self-immolation. Fake 25-rouble notes have been found that were entirely hand-drawn with coloured pencils. They are genuine works of art that obviously required several days of filigree work to perfect. (Investigations are focused on retirees from the Fine Art Academy.)

Other hotshots soak the new 10-rouble notes in a chemical solution which softens the ink. Then, using a double pressing against plastic laminated sheets, they literally print a new note. (Investigations are focused on the university chemistry departments.)

And it's not just the banknotes. The coins are a headache too. The one-, two- and three-kopeck coins in the old style have remained in circulation at their face value. Mathematical geniuses have immediately deduced that their purchasing power will automatically be multiplied by ten. All you have to do to make a fortune is convert your old roubles into very small change and wait a bit. With the result that from one day to the next, not a single one of these coins is in circulation in the entire country.

There's a story going round about a homeless woman from the provinces, who had the foresight to accumulate small change in milk cans for ten years, and then suddenly found herself in possession of vast wealth.

People exaggerate, fantasise, imagine all sorts of things.

Even so, getting rid of speculators is a priority.

General mobilisation!

The most urgent task: any person found in possession of more than one hundred coins, either at home or in their pockets, is charged. The money is confiscated, then returned once it's been converted at the official rate.

The time you waste on these footling tasks! It's wearying. But it has to be done. If you let the taste for profit develop, even on this small scale, then… then… the radiant future will go down the drain.

Speculation, the enemy of genuine work, has no place in the home of socialism.

All of a sudden, you can't ignore it any longer, you can see it, it's huge! The black market is right there in your face. It's the only thing anyone talks about. Was it the currency reform that acted as a catalyst? Or did the parasites just become too arrogant after basking in impunity for so long?

The fact of the matter is that crowds of scoundrels gather on the riverbank, around the big hotels, at the airport, on Gorky Street – there's wheeling and dealing going on everywhere.

Foreigners are systematically approached by bold young people propositioning them with all kinds of deals. Tourists from the West can sell their scarves, ties, shoes, socks, underwear, lighters, ballpoint pens, lipstick (even used), half empty cologne bottles, any old junk – they are department stores unto themselves. If they wanted to, in a few minutes, they could sell literally everything they are wearing, and go home stark naked.

Foreign currency is utter madness. Speculators buy it from tourists at an unbeatable rate, far superior to the State's. Then they sell it to those Russians who are allowed to travel abroad (sportsmen, performers), but can only exchange the equivalent of thirty dollars officially.

"That's still thirty dollars too many," Shmakov grumbles. "They shouldn't be coveting all that gimcrackery produced abroad by the sweat of the proletariat."

When the Competent Authority finally started to realise what was going on, what came as a surprise, an enormous surprise, was the extent and the depth of the gangrene.

In Gorky Street you find only the little wankers, the "runners".

The dollars they buy are resold to more experienced

guys, the "chiefs". Who resell them in turn to the "dealers". The "kings" are those at the very top of the pyramid. They don't go anywhere for less than ten thousand roubles.

The sums involved are unfathomable.

To think that Ivanov earns 120 roubles a month!

Of course he does get the bonus of vouchers for exclusive and confidential suppliers, and mind-boggling discounts on holiday packages, and free housing, and a transport card, and a red I.D. card that gets him to the head of any queue.

He can't complain.

Paradoxically, with all that money, it's the king who is stuck. In the land of socialism, luxury is something of a relative notion. You can't buy an apartment or a car with two toots of your horn like they do in the West. As for the shops, it's not that they're empty, it's just that you never know in advance what you might find there.

Sure, you can stuff your face like a combine harvester at fancy restaurants like the National or the Aragvi. To get in the door of those mythical places, you have to be either a Party boss or an actor-footballer-chess-player-circus-director. Plebs get sternly turned away unless they drop a 25-rouble note in the bouncer's paw. Make sure you have another 25-rouble note for the waitress if you don't want her to be rude and arrogant. By discreetly showing his little red I.D. booklet, Ivanov can get in whenever he wants. But the place is always packed with V.I.P.s drinking heavily: the atmosphere can sour quickly and end up getting a low-ranking nobody like him into hot water.

Nikonovich is emphatic: you should avoid those sorts of places at all costs, unless you're a colonel (or higher), or you're on a mission.

Money! There's never enough of it, but when you have too much of it, you can't actually spend it – what a great country we live in!

If you really want to blow your dough, you pay a gofer to stand in queues at the shops for you. For the heavy stuff (T.V., fridge), when the waiting time is measured in months, you can cut a deal with a mate whose number is at the head of the queue. Without ever being sure that you'll actually get your hands on the coveted merchandise.

Shmakov thinks this is wonderful.

"Any arsehole can put a gold brick on the table, but his Volga sedan won't get made any faster when there's a shortage of sheet metal at the factory!"

A gold brick is a figure of speech of course, for if a citizen should openly do such a thing, the Competent Authority would be notified at once. We would deal with him under a microscope, and without anaesthetic, you can be sure of that!

As for foreign currency, it's quite simple, really. Being in possession of any at one's home, without being able to justify it by having work abroad, is a crime.

The "kings" are forced to keep their cash in suitcases that they leave in left luggage offices – for fear of being caught during a house search.

Like Yan Rokotov. This individual, whom we quickly identified by infiltrating the network and tailing him, is one of those "kings". In fact he is the king of kings.

We arrested him as he was collecting a suitcase from a left luggage counter (the time limit was up).

Altogether, the guy had a total of $16,000 dollars' worth of gold, jewels and foreign currency.

An immeasurable amount.

In the Soviet Union, it's easier to do a back handspring than to spend even a tenth of that sum.

Which is why this country is morally superior to capitalist society. And its athletes and acrobats and dancers are the best in the world.

Here anyone who gets rich ends up like Midas, drowning under their gold.

Yan Rokotov takes a rather nonchalant attitude to his trial. He's up for a maximum of eight years, but he willingly answers the judge's questions, and teases the prosecutor. He declares: "As far as communist society goes, I don't think it can be built within two thousand years, in other words ever. Which is a way of saying that I don't believe in the idea of the construction of Communism at all."

Along with his two accomplices, he gets the maximum penalty, obviously. Eight years in a labour camp.

Shmakov is livid.

"That's not justice, that's taking the piss! Eight measly years? That's a cockroach's fart!"

Captain Nikonovich tries to reason with him.

"It's the maximum allowed in the Criminal Code. You can't load the boat with more than what is written in the law."

Shmakov won't hear of it.

"He refuses to work like the rest of us? In the old days… thwack!"

Khrushchev is on exactly the same wavelength. Some metalworkers wrote him a letter that he found very moving: "Eight years in a labour camp – that's too lenient! We simple Soviet workers ask you solemnly to show no pity to those scumbags, those miserable degenerates, that filthy trash whose vile souls are empty, but who have become more and more arrogant and no longer respect the Soviet system. They are worse than traitors, they have been corpses for a long time, and we ask you to make an example of them by sentencing the whole criminal gang to capital punishment. So that they don't sully the incorruptible reputation of the Soviet people, so that they no longer breathe the same air as us, so that they can no longer call themselves citizens of the U.S.S.R."

Captain Nikonovich, who knows Khrushchev's rhetorical style very well (he's responsible for producing a précis of every Central Committee speech for the staff), wonders if the general secretary didn't pen this noose of a letter himself. He doesn't breathe a word of this suspicion to anyone, of course.

Whether those metalworkers exist or not, you can understand how they would feel.

The population's outrage rises up at these "corpses", who are still very much alive.

The magistrates quickly rewrite the law: now you can get fifteen years. The Ministry appeals, and Yan Rokotov, already convicted according to the previous law, sees his sentence increased to fifteen years.

Shmakov grinds his teeth.

"He was fucking lucky."

Fifteen years is better than eight, of course, but it's not as good as the death sentence.

Khrushchev is furious: "The judges themselves should be judged for such lenient sentences!"

That message is read loud and clear.

As a matter of urgency, the law is rewritten a second time. Yan Rokotov is sentenced to death.

Khrushchev receives his request for clemency, written in a shaky hand.

"I am sentenced to be shot. My crime is to have speculated in foreign currency and gold coins. Twice, the retroactive force of the law has been applied to me, retrospectively. I beg you to let me live. I have made many mistakes. Now I am being reborn as a completely different person. I am thirty-three years old, I will be a useful citizen of the Soviet state. I am not a murderer or a spy, after all. Now that my mind has been cleared, I want to live and to construct Communism with the Soviet people. I beg you to take pity on me."

Dream on!

He is shot. His mates too.

Retroactively and "as an exceptional case". To set an example.

That sends a chill around the foreign currency speculators.

The taste of blood spreads through the Competent Authority.

Despite all the arguments to do with public opinion in the West, which we must not offend (quoth Nikonovich), sometimes Ivanov, contaminated by Shmakov's enthusiasm, wonders why they didn't do the same thing with Pasternak.

"For literature?" Larissa wonders.

She is just finishing the darning. The lightbulb she uses to stretch the fabric of the sock by slipping it inside it goes back into the clever housewife's tin mending box.

"It's a severe penalty, I agree. But a logical one. At least that way we wouldn't have ended up with Abram Tertz."

"There's not an Abram Tertz on every street corner. He's a lone wolf, so to speak. Whereas there are hundreds of currency dealers. Come on, don't be grumpy. I know you're not a bloodthirsty baby ogre. Otherwise I would not have wedded thee."

Ivanov pretends to disagree.

"I have a shadow side too, you know. Sometimes I just wish I could… We've just discovered a spicy piece of information about Abram Tertz."

"Stop! You're not supposed to tell me anything about the investigation. It's classified Secret."

"We've finally found out where the name comes from. A sarge who's an expert on common criminals has just filled us in. Apparently there's a song that gangsters in Odessa sing that goes like this: "Abrashka Tertz, the pickpocket of legend, and Sonya-the-whore, who shines throughout the land.""

A pickpocket. A whore. That scoundrel who dared to criticise socialist realism chose a pen name from a song about street lowlife.

That means he's probably done time in the Gulag. To know those sorts of songs you have to have the right C.V. Maybe that's a lead. Alas for the investigators, in a country which has just lived through the post-Stalinist amnesty and the mass return of convicts, there's no shortage of former inmates.

These ideas get jotted down in a notebook. Next to the words "Poland" and "Jewish" are added "former *zek*". And "Odessa", followed by a question mark.

VI

The mission of the Competent Authority is clear.

It is set down in black and white in Minutes no. 200, dated January 9, 1959, compiled after the meeting of the Presidium of the Central Committee of the Communist Party of the Soviet Union.

"The K.G.B. is a political organ implementing the decisions of the Central Committee of the Party with regard to the security of the socialist State confronted with the attacks from its external and internal enemies.

"The duty of this organ is to monitor attentively the secret attempts by the enemies of the Soviet Union, to uncover their plans, and to put a term to the heinous activities of the imperialist intelligence agencies."

This leads to a healthy attitude of mistrust towards the whole world.

If you thought that the country we live in is the largest on the planet, you'd be wrong: the Soviet Union is an island. A plot of land lost in a hostile ocean. A patch of clarity in an endless stretch of toxic water. Water which is rising, and seeks only to rise higher, to erase our land from the surface of the globe. A besieged island fighting the dark forces of worldwide imperialism.

There are dykes protecting our country from annihilation. An impermeable belt around the coastline is essential to our survival. A well-guarded border is not a luxury. You do not enter into the land of the future as you would walk into a barn!

Out there in the fetid water, there are sharks and octopuses swimming. How happy they would be for the Soviet Union to disappear! You can almost feel their covetous looks, their panting breath. You might think they are asleep, but in fact they are on the prowl, seeking out the slightest weakness.

They did, as early as 1917. Then in 1918, in 1919… They came a cropper a few times, back then. But did that make them pull back their tentacles? Oh no, not a bit! Look at Budapest in 1956. A pseudo-revolt fomented by Western agents. Would any population of sane mind consider leaving the bosom of the march towards socialism? We had to get tough. Send out faithful leucocytes to fight the infection.

The Competent Authority – the immune system of the Fatherland. It's a fine image. And a fairly accurate one too. Like digestive enzymes, Lieutenant Ivanov and his comrades are invisible yet effective guards. They defend the organism with their shield, eradicate enemies with their sword. The healthy body doesn't even realise that these devoted sentries are there keeping watch over it day and night. The citizens go about their daily lives – protected. Go shopping – protected. Go to the cinema with a spring in their step – protected. While in the shadows, the immune system is always on red alert.

An encounter with a stranger? An anti-Soviet book? An inappropriate joke? So many potential entryways for a dangerous microbe. That's where the Competent Authority intervenes. The intruder is identified, followed, studied. You assimilate its tactics. Then you eliminate it. While keeping an eye on any metastases, which are always possible. God only knows what might happen to healthy cells that come into contact with the virus.

"Your summary is excellent, comrade Ivanov," Colonel Volkov gushes. "I would even say it is exalting!"

He rises from his seat and, flouting protocol, walks around the table and embraces Ivanov.

When usually he never even deigns to smile!

"I'm giving you the top mark."

Lieutenant Ivanov is thrilled. That's what you call a successfully conducted performance appraisal.

He leaves the human resource management office on a little cloud.

It's not that he was worried, no, he knows the hierarchy is satisfied with his work, but still, you can never be too sure. Especially since "polit-prep" is a treacherous discipline – you have to keep up with the Party's latest obsessions.

The previous week, he had read *Pravda* and *Izvestia* assiduously every morning.

The thing about the immune system came to him when he saw someone cough on a packed trolleybus. Why do the other passengers not immediately fall ill?

The work of the leucocytes. The work of the Competent Authority.

The lieutenant did not remind the colonel that all this work is carried out at the peril of one's own personal comfort. The zealous leucocyte does not have an easy life. It loses track of the number of weekends it is unable to spend with its family. Ivanov has the distinct impression that his son, when he is born, if ever he is born, will grow up without him. If his relationship with Larissa is holding up, it's probably only because her father was in the military, and often absent on prolonged missions in the Far North. She knows all about separations.

And what can you say about the trips to the provinces, when you are sometimes forced to sleep in unheated shacks? Or out into the countryside, where you have to shit outside, even at $-20°C$, squatting over the hole in the outhouse? And how can you not be exhausted by those interminable stakeouts when you're asked to lend a hand to the operations branch, those long days spent in hiding, when the body seizes up like a wheelbarrow left lying on its side?

Once, because there wasn't a bed in the hovel he was sheltering in, and he wasn't about to lie down to sleep in the freezing mud spread all over the floor, he took a door off its hinges and set it up so it was balanced between two chairs. With only his officer's coat as a mattress, with a few wet branches as padding, he could have been mistaken for a hermit in hibernation.

Ivanov is proud to keep these gloomy thoughts to himself.

A week later, Lieutenant Ivanov learns that he has been assigned to the position of Deputy to Investigator Pakhmonov.

In the eighth directorate, he is now one of the lieutenants to watch.

His colleagues ask him for advice. His superiors enquire about his goals – where does he see his career heading?

It is clear, however – given his mediocre results in pistol

shooting – that he is not cut out to be a field operative.

"Taking care of anti-Soviet propaganda suits me perfectly," he replies. "There is so much to do! Clearing out the weeds, over and over again."

And so modest with it!

Is it any surprise, then, that he is invited shortly afterwards to attend one of Shelepin's speeches in person?

"The State security organs have been successfully reorganised," says the man with steely eyes and an immaculate suit. "Staff numbers have been significantly reduced. The free riders have been asked to move on. The Competent Authority is no longer the scarecrow that Beria, not so long ago, thought it should be. We are now an integral component of the Party. Today all Cheka officers can have a clear conscience. They can look the Party and the Soviet people squarely in the eye."

The renewal of the Competent Authority, that's him, Ivanov, sitting there in the fifteenth row.

The lieutenant comes out with his head swollen bigger than ever. "It's worth the fight, worth giving it one's all!" There seems to be something like a warm updraft.

And not just in Ivanov's career.

VII

In April 1961, the astonished galaxy discovers *Pravda*'s headline, printed in huge red letters.

"A phenomenal milestone in the history of humankind!"

Time stands still for Ivanov, Kulakov and Nikonovich. Work grinds to a halt. Surveillance slackens. The tails drop off. The typewriters fall silent.

Still in red, the words underneath tumble over each other, jump out all at once, suddenly punch drunk:

"A world first, the Soviet spaceship Vostok completed an orbit of the Earth with a man on board, and returned safe and sound to the sacred soil of our Fatherland."

World first.

Soviet.

The sacred soil of our Fatherland.

Then they all calm down a bit, get a grip on their emotions:

"The first man to go into space is a citizen of the Union of Soviet Socialist Republics, Yuri Alexeyevich Gagarin."

Capital letters all over the page. Exclamation points like splashes of summer rain.

Out in the streets, people are euphoric, laughing for no reason. Some start singing.

An impromptu crowd has cobbled together some banners and is wandering about quite freely, with no official sanction. "THE COSMOS IS OURS!" "MOSCOW – COSMOS – MOSCOW! HURRAH!" "WE ARE THE FIRST!"

Young people are shouting so much that you wonder whether you shouldn't go and break it all up and disperse the crowd, but the orders are issued, categorically: let popular jubilation be expressed.

And jubilation it is.

An unquestionable victory of the socialist system. Take that, you imperialists! We proved we are the best! One in your eye! And everywhere else! Up to the hilt!

First there was Sputnik. Now Vostok.

When a nation is united by an ideal, the laws of gravitation no longer apply. That people produced a superhero: Gagarin.

Before being sent into space, he was selected, then tested and re-tested. A meticulous investigation, which the Competent Authority took charge of, explored his family and friends. What if he had been the son of a convict, or had noble ancestors, or a Jewish root or two? The superhero must be Russian, above all else. And politically reliable.

His pedigree is perfect: he comes from a family of country bumpkins working in a kolkhoz. One of his grandfathers was a worker at the Putilov arms factory where the February 1917 Revolution began. The other was a farm labourer and carpenter. A pure-blooded communist.

A wife, two children. Member of the Party for one year – that's essential.

Obedient, compliant, smiling. Always prepared! Like a mutt you take out for its evening walk. Enough to make you wonder whether the superhero isn't just a bit thick. He'd have to be, to accept being propelled into space in a white-hot tin can.

His chances of survival were estimated to be 50 per cent. Heads you die burnt to a crisp, tails you hit the massive jackpot. Did he consider this? No, of course not, this simple lad doesn't care a jot about personal gain.

But still. The jackpot is bigger than anyone could imagine. Once the initial euphoria dies down, it's back to work: the Competent Authority is charged with implementing a memorandum issued by the Council of Ministers, classified Secret, and titled "Regarding the recompense for Comrade Gagarin for having accomplished a special mission in exemplary fashion". Absolute confidentiality must be guaranteed.

Its contents are explosive.

The grateful nation is offering the first man in space its finest, most rare and precious goods. A large sum of money (15,000 roubles), a three-bedroom apartment (fully furnished), a Volga car, a television set, a Soviet Luxe brand radio (with built-in turntable), a vacuum cleaner. As well as a "rig-out" like a bride's trousseau, comprising the following items:

Mid-weight coat – 1 unit
Lightweight summer coat – 1 unit
Raincoat – 1 unit
Suit – 2 units (one dark, one light)
Shoes – 2 pairs (one black, one tan)
White shirt – 6 units
Hat – 2 units
Tie – 6 units

Gloves – 1 pair
Handkerchief – 12 units
Socks – 6 pairs
Underpants, vests – 6 pairs
Electric razor – 1 unit.

The hero's wife has not been forgotten either: six pairs of stockings, two housecoats, two scarves, one jumper... Nor have his parents and children.

Goods coveted by the entire population.

You can imagine the ridicule in the West if this list, signed by Nikita Khrushchev in person, fell into a journalist's hands. The glaring nakedness of a country with chronic shortages of basic goods (socks, vests) would be exposed to the prurient gaze of international derision.

It's not that you can never find shirts, gloves or ties in the shops. They are there, subject to deliveries. But getting hold of them when you actually need them, and in the right size and quantity, is something of a supernatural feat, above all in the provinces.

The Competent Authority is mobilised. The public servants sent out on the treasure hunt must be accompanied. You make telephone calls, knock on the doors of the Politburo's reserved stocks, assess the quality of the fabrics, finger the leather. A guy from the staff who is exactly the same size as Gagarin has to do all the trying-on. For the wife and parents, it's not so critical. They can fix their stuff up a bit. When everything is given to you for free, you don't make a fuss.

Within forty-eight hours, the whole caboodle is collected and ready.

Mission accomplished!

The superhero now has an electric razor.

It's the least we could do. He deserved it. If only for having made all those capitalist countries fall off their chairs. Never since the death of Stalin has the Soviet Union been at the centre of the world like this, at the heart of progress. An avalanche of favourable articles, including in America! Gagarin is acclaimed, given medals by everybody, invited on a worldwide tour. Admirers of the world, unite!

The morale of the leucocytes is galvanised.

Who cares about Pasternak when we have Gagarin?

Kulakov, beaming from ear to ear, cuts out the headline from *Izvestia* and pins it up inside his locker. "Huge victory for our government, our science, our technology, our bravery!" Every morning, he drinks strength from this fountain of truth.

"We must be worthy of Gagarin!" he starts saying on a regular basis, thumping his chest with his open palm.

He was always a tad daft, that Kulakov.

But now, with renewed energy, the team rolls up its sleeves. Including Erika – as if Vostok's success had given her a new spring in her mechanism. Never before has she typed so accurately and so fast.

I'll get you, Abram Tertz! Ivanov thinks as he summarises the foreign reports, from which it becomes clear that the distribution of "The Trial Begins" is still spreading. Translations are blossoming everywhere. Even more worrying: a new blip has appeared on the radar of anti-Soviet publications, one Nikolai Arzhak, who has published a brief short story, where? In *Kultura* magazine, for a change. It has to be the same channel.

It's called "The Hands". The chilling story of a doughty

Cheka officer whose hands start shaking as he is about to execute a priest at close range. He fires, misses, fires again, misses again. Just as in a bad dream. At the end of the story, it all becomes clear: his mischievous comrades had played a practical joke on him, by loading his Nagant with blanks.

Just a few pages, narrated in the first person. And an uneasy feeling for Ivanov – as if this Arzhak had accused him of being personally responsible for the terror of the first years of the Revolution, or of sharing an intertemporal complicity with Felix Dzerzhinsky, the shadowy genius of the Cheka, whose bust sits enthroned at the entrance to the building.

Surprise surprise, Kolya Arzhak is also a gangster's name. In the song about him, Kolya Arzhak, armed only with a broken bottle, fights alone against a gang of fourteen thugs, and of course bleeds out, "for he doesn't deserve to live, if he was so stupid as to go out without a knife".

So, Abram Tertz has whelped a pup.

The same channel to smuggle the stuff out, the same typology in the signature. Those two know each other. If we can get one, we'll get the other.

Tertz, Arzhak: together they have apparently defined a new literary micro-movement, just like that. At least that's what all the Western journals are claiming. They call it "*fantastic* realism", in contrast, of course, to socialist realism. Putting a stop to all this is now a matter of urgency.

Forward, leucocytes!

Long live Gagarin!

VIII

Caged alive in the Soviet embassy in Paris, a glass of Chablis in hand, Jean-Marie Domenach is bored around the bend. These cultural receptions are so tedious! He only accepted the invitation because he was hoping to meet Ilya Ehrenburg, that writer with a gift of ubiquity and matchless longevity, whose memoirs, *People, Years, Life* are due to be published by Gallimard in a few months' time.

Ehrenburg made it through the hailstorm of Stalinism without feeling a drop – as if the man had diabolical powers. He knew Modigliani, Apollinaire, Joyce, Lenin, Bukharin and the rest, he speaks *haute-couture* French, but Domenach will not be seeing him tonight. A bad flu, explains the embarrassed cultural attaché to all the "left-leaning" French literati who have been invited to the occasion.

"Ilya Grigoryevich has a fever of 39 degrees. He was not able to fly."

To compensate for this loss, some entertainment has been arranged. Extracts of Ehrenburg's book are read aloud, then translated ad lib.

Domenach, who has a mole at Gallimard, has already read the collection – which is as fascinating in what it reveals as it is frustrating in what it does not. So many corpses strewn between the lines, so many ghosts haunting the counter spaces of the letters! Some pages feel like a ramble through an abandoned cemetery. Bucolic and terrifying.

A face with a muddy complexion approaches.

"Do not be concerned in the slightest, Monsieur Domenach, Ilya Grigoryevich comes next month, as soon as he feels better."

Ropey French but an impeccably tailored suit. Cufflinks. Pocket square. Silver cigarette holder.

"No thank you, I don't smoke lights," Domenach says.

"Vladimir Vinogradov, at your service."

This is followed by small talk in which the two men exchange their knowledge of Chablis and its climate.

"Fourchaume, in *premier cru*, this year remarkable," Vinogradov says. "Alas, little too pricey for our pockets at embassy. This evening we Petit Chablis drink."

"There are some great Petits Chablis," Domenach says sagely.

Vinogradov entirely agrees.

They have another glass. Then another.

This Vinogradov is very friendly. And he's in a good mood. He is in charge of the sales of all Russian export goods. That's huge.

"Caviar and vodka are (how you say?) anecdotic in our turnover. We sell most wood, minerals, wheat. And soon maize."

"Corn?" Domenach is surprised.

"National priority. In Western Siberia, production of corn multiplied by ten. New lands. Magnificent. In maize production, we plan (but, careful, is top secret), we plan catch up U.S.A. by 1967."

Domenach looks stunned. But why not corn, after all?

Another glass of Chablis later, Domenach starts telling funny jokes about Khrushchev.

"So someone asks Nikita Khrushchev if it's true that soon, once Communism is installed, they'll be able to order their shopping over the telephone. And Khrushchev replies: 'Of course! And it'll be delivered through the T.V.!'"

Vinogradov laughs heartily. Then:

"One confidence deserves another. Tell me, that Abram Tertz… So funny. I read his little pamphlet. And I must say I was disappointed. Yes, disappointed. It is (how you say) a hoax, yes?"

"What do you mean, a hoax?"

"Admit it. It was émigré from here who wrote the piece. Probably White Russian. Who is pretending to be Soviet. Classic move to get publicity."

"No, it wasn't!" Domenach protests vigorously.

That Vinogradov seems to be accusing him of conspiring in committing intellectual fraud, no less.

Domenach is outraged.

"The manuscript came to us from the Soviet Union. I am certain of it!"

"That's impossible." Vinogradov chuckles. "There are turns of phrase that give it away. It is hoax."

"I can assure you it did! I have proof."

Vinogradov tenses up a bit, all smiles. His eyes become pointy. His ears multiply. Speak! He wants to yell. Come on, you nitwit, tell me! Tell Daddy everything. Give me your sources, for God's sake!

And then Domenach, with an air of perfect imbecility, says: "One morning, the manuscript arrived in the post, just like that. The package had been posted in the U.S.S.R. From Leningrad, I think."

And he sees Vinogradov's face fall apart.

"In the post?!?"

You thought I was an idiot, well there you go! Domenach exults, faced with his interlocutor's despairing expression.

"Well, yes, in the post. But what's wrong, Monsieur Vinogradov? You look lost all of a sudden. That Petit Chablis can be treacherous."

Domenach is of course aware that it is impossible to send a letter to France without it going past the censorship services, who open everything and read everything.

Vinogradov likewise is aware of this.

But these are not services that the Soviet state wishes to brag about.

The envelopes are steamed in a vertical tower, made in Czechoslovakia. Then it's easy to pull away the softened flaps with a bone paper knife. Before reading them, you have to wash your hands so you don't leave any traces (be careful of postmarks that bleed!). Then you put it all back together with ordinary postal glue, which you apply with a paintbrush.

Sometimes the machine gets blocked by an envelope sealed with some kind of rustic glue, homemade by the sender. Then you take the time to pass it to the "chemist", who can do anything. And if you have to tear it a little to open it up, well then you just tear it! Then you slap a blue stamp on the envelope: "Item damaged in transit. Re-glued by the postal service." But in French, if you please. Because French is the official language of the Universal Postal Union.

Letters in foreign languages are sorted by country and submitted to the sagacity of bilingual employees.

The basic rule is this: better for a letter to get lost than to show traces of having been opened.

One day, thinking he would fool the Competent Authority, a prankster put his letter through a sewing machine, connecting the envelope and its contents with a web of thread. Impossible to open the letter quickly without tearing the whole thing apart. The agents' curiosity was all the more piqued. They took the time to snip off each stitch: two days of surgery. They studied the contents then threw the whole lot into the rubbish – it was just impossible to put it back together again as if it were untouched.

Vinogradov knows all that.

It can be only one of two possibilities. Either Abram Tertz really did arrive in the West through the post – that seems impossible, but why not, we're not machines after all. An unbelievable stroke of luck.

Or this Domenach guy is playing him for a fool.

"Well, I've got to go," Domenach says with a wide smile. "Hope to see you again sometime!"

That very evening, Vinogradov compiles his potentially explosive report. How is it possible that the Leningrad postal service is so remiss in its operations? he asks.

This raises quite a few eyebrows in Moscow, on those whom it may concern.

An urgent investigation is launched. One hundred letters with subversive contents are posted in one hundred post boxes throughout the Leningrad area. Destination: France. How many will be caught in the vigilant nets?

A week later, everyone is reassured. The findings

indicate that the work is being carried out correctly, overall. The interception rate is flawless: all the litigious letters were identified and opened. However, the analysis of the contents could be improved. While the vast majority were blocked, twelve letters were not duly analysed all the way to the end (carelessness, dereliction of duty) and were authorised to continue on their journey.

On the balance of probabilities, Abram Tertz did not get to France through the post.

There remains the question of provenance: Leningrad. Domenach, thinking he was making a mockery of the Competent Authority, has let slip a vital clue.

Lieutenant Ivanov sets out for Leningrad. He stays there long enough to reactivate his informants. The patient little bee visits all the flowers in his garden.

The investigator has requested that all efforts focus squarely on Leningrad. The files of every professor, teacher, writer or scientist who may have spent time in Poland, or had contact with Polish people, go to the top of the pile. Around a hundred names (with priority given to those of Jewish origin) are the subject of careful monitoring.

The process always starts with a proximity investigation: you discreetly interrogate their neighbours and colleagues. You draw up a chart of the circles the target moves in and their interests.

The exercise may seem tedious, but it always pays off in the long run. And you find out all sorts of things! An eminent ethnographer owns several copies of *Doctor Zhivago* – which he rents out by the week to make ends meet. (Four years in a labour camp.) A doctoral student in history, of Polish origin, has the impertinence to conduct personal research on the Katyn massacre, and is compiling a special notebook of the accounts by Byelorussian peasants. (Immediate expulsion from the university. Her father, the dean of the music faculty, is dismissed shortly afterwards.)

Sometimes, when looking at his chart of names where those of potentially culpable citizens are circled in red, Lieutenant Ivanov feels within himself the soul of a goatherd. He selects and grooms the good animals, eliminates the corruptible ones, keeps watch on his flock. It's his duty, his responsibility. "What a beautiful city Leningrad is!" he writes to Larissa on the back of a postcard of the Smolny Institute, Lenin's headquarters during the Revolution. She responds with an illustration by Evgeny Gundobin, "The Philately Lesson". He could just see himself as that idyllic grandfather, all solid moustachioed benevolence, showing his stamp collection to two adorable toddlers. And thus, between two goat delousing sessions, the lieutenant's heart swells with tenderness.

IX

While waiting for his arrest, Abram Tertz attends a soporific seminar at the I.M.L.I., the prestigious Institute of World Literature, in Moscow.

As he sits there pretending to listen to the speaker talking about Soviet authors' successes in foreign countries – Sholokhov blah blah blah – the dangerous hooligan counts up the years of his miraculous freedom. Five years and two months since he first sent his writing to the West. Two years and seven months since *Esprit*. And still nothing. No summons to the offices of the Competent Authority. As if he had done nothing at all.

Far from savouring this feeling of impunity and strutting arrogantly about, Abram Tertz is regularly liquidised by flushes of anxiety. For him, the great specialist of Dostoyevsky, it's *Crime and Punishment* every day.

He's lucid about it. He knows that the inescapable outcome is staring him in the face.

If the law didn't knock on his door yesterday, it will today.

Or tomorrow.

His cushy life as a professor and literary critic will come to an end.

Ilya Ehrenburg can say what he likes about a "thaw"

in the novel he published after the Ogre's demise, Abram Tertz cannot feel his toes anymore for the cold.

Thaw, my arse!

It's not that *The Thaw* is bad, it's more that it's written in prose that stinks of Soviet bureaucracy, even if it does contain a few timid allusions to the "excesses" of the glacial years.

If thaw means no longer executing hundreds of thousands of innocent people, well then, sure, thaw. Heatwave, even.

Except that thaw doesn't mean the guilty will be treated kindly. Abram Tertz shudders. Absolutely not! The culprit, thaw or not, must be caught and punished.

And Abram Tertz is most certainly guilty.

Judge for yourselves, ye honest citizens, the incredible splash of pride that compelled him to want to show his writing to other readers besides his desk drawer!

Behold how the criminal then hands over two of his manuscripts to his French friend, Hélène Peltier, with the mission of exfiltrating them out of his country.

Hélène is as clever as she is utterly devoted. Eyes sparkling with malice, natural grace, intoxicating poise. How could you not fall in love with her? In 1947 Hélène came to cultivate her passion for Russian literature on the benches of the University of Moscow. The daughter of a military attaché at the French Embassy, trapped in the Soviet Union for as long as her father was on manoeuvres here, she was twenty-three years old and the man who was not yet Abram Tertz was twenty-two.

You should have seen her shine among the awkward, uncouth, inhibited Russian girls! Her merest gesture had the exotic, slightly incongruous elegance of a pink flamingo. When there weren't enough chairs for everybody at a party, she would swirl her skirt around and sit on the floor, perfectly relaxed at the feet of our enthralled young men, as if this was the most natural thing in the world.

Winter 1947. That biting cold…

She did not wither.

With the thaw, she even came back.

In the meantime, Abram Tertz had married. Twice. Clearly, a hooligan.

In August 1956, Hélène takes his manuscripts to send them to France. Conscious of the risks, she mobilises all her wits and never underestimates her adversary, whom she knows to be devious and endowed with an invisibility cape.

She still has contacts at the embassy. A friend she can be sure of. She hands her a sealed envelope, which will leave the country in the diplomatic pouch.

When she collects the package in Paris, instead of rushing straight to all the publishing houses, she takes her time choosing her targets. Saint-Germain-des-Prés is so full of chatterboxes! So indulgent towards the Soviet Union! She must not put the existence of her dear Abram Tertz at risk by confiding in the wrong people.

One thing is certain: if she is identified as the mule, Abram Tertz is done for. All the Competent Authority will have to do is go through Hélène Peltier's file: her contacts have been duly listed there. You don't let a daughter of a French military attaché wander the streets of Moscow without strict surveillance.

She takes two years to approach Domenach and to dissect him. Can she trust this man who never looks at you when he talks, yet speaks in a clear emphatic voice? To test him, she drops names, "Pasternak", "Ehrenburg", and takes note of his reactions.

"While the bloodthirsty character of the regime changed with Stalin's death, its repressive nature and its relationship with ideology have not changed one iota," Domenach tells her. "Ehrenburg is a phony. The thaw is a mask. Look at the fangs and the grey tail sticking out." Very few intellectuals are this discerning.

It will be Domenach then. Hélène shows him the manuscript, he's thrilled. They come to an agreement: maximum camouflage. The manuscript of *On Socialist Realism* will arrive at *Esprit*'s office by the post just like any other – that way no-one, not even the mailroom staff will guess that the source was one of Domenach's personal contacts. Hélène's name will not be mentioned anywhere and there will be no return address on the envelope.

During their conversations about Abram Tertz, Hélène makes a point of insisting that everything happened in Leningrad. "When I was in Leningrad…" "Tertz loves art. The Hermitage is like a second home to him." "Have you ever been to Leningrad?"

She and Abram Tertz had discussed this, speaking softly on a park bench, in a conspiratorial mood, their armpits dripping.

"Let's throw some sequins up into the air to disorient the bird."

If you want half a chance to carry on, you need to send the enemy off on false trails, keep them busy, confuse them.

A geographical decoy: Leningrad. A cultural decoy: let's pretend there is a connection with Poland. And to top it all off, an ethnic decoy: he will be Jewish! Absolutely one hundred per cent Jewish. Never has a Russian tried to pass as a Jew – that would be nothing short of perversion in a country where anti-Semitism is endemic.

In Abram Tertz's passport, just as in every Soviet citizen's, after his family name, given name, patronymic, and date of birth, a fifth line gives his ethnic origin. And when you are "Jewish" on that terrible fifth line, you are discriminated against at school, at university, in the workplace, where a "Russian" of comparably inferior achievement will always be given preference.

"In this country, it's an honour to be Jewish when you're Russian," Abram Tertz declares.

As for Poland, the opportunity makes the thief. Hélène had married the Polish sculptor August Zamoyski. A family of impeccable nobility, who have contacts at *Kultura*, the Polish dissident journal. They are trustworthy people, who know the value of discretion. He could offer a piece of writing to them first, it would be an excellent debut.

The crime was thus premeditated and meticulously considered. Compared to Tertz the cold-blooded criminal, Raskolnikov was an impulsive amateur.

And it is because the crime was thought through beforehand down to the smallest details that Abram Tertz is still free.

Behold the scandal: there he is, sitting in the second row, surrounded by twenty or so other writers.

On the stage, a tiresome brunette is droning through her presentation. Short-legged, wearing a dress with big drab flowers that looks as if it was cut out of an old bedspread – she looks just like our contemporary literature, Abram

Tertz thinks. Insipid, barely rising off the ground, heavy-footed, crushing everything in its path.

The brunette starts reading the annual report of the previous year in a flat voice. Theme of the day: the commercial success of the "Made in U.S.S.R." label applied to literature. How do our writers get distributed in export markets? Not a word about Pasternak, obviously. But Sholokhov, on the other hand… Abram Tertz stifles a yawn. When suddenly:

"With some delay, and in case this information might be of some use, we must report the publication in the West of a detestable pamphlet. It is called *On Socialist Realism*."

Like a pin stuck into his shoulder blade!

The culprit is instantly flushed to his hairline and his ears are blinking – a feeling of dizziness.

Now, now, calm down! No-one suspects that it's you.

The speaker is not looking at him specifically. In fact it even seems as if she's ignoring him.

When he is right there in front of her, like a boil popping out from the palm of your hand, trembling, and… exhilarated.

Without noticing anything suspicious, the brunette continues:

"The author is hiding under the pseudonym of Abram Tertz. The pamphlet has been reprinted by a dozen reactionary journals, including *Esprit, Kultura, Encounter*."

Jeepers! *Encounter* too! That's crazy, just crazy!

He knew about *Esprit* and *Kultura* from a postcard Hélène sent him with these enigmatic words on the back – enigmatic for everyone except them: "Paris is yours, Warsaw too!"

He understands: this is it, he is published in the West!

The water leaking from the fifth floor of the building has finally seeped down to the first, he thinks, admiring the rosette on the ceiling.

Getting slapped in the face with the official confirmation of your criminal nature, in the middle of a public I.M.L.I. meeting, does shake you up a bit.

"We will have to draw the necessary consequences, dear Comrades," the brunette warns.

In other words, be vigilant. Keep your eyes open. Be ready to rebuff the traitor and his Western puppeteers with strongly worded articles in which we can rise up as one to defend the vilified Fatherland.

But we are not at that point yet.

"It is possible that it's a hoax. A fake, written in France by an émigré. Several hypotheses are being considered. The Competent Authority is working on the case. To give you an idea of the contents, here are a few significant extracts."

And the voice of Abram Tertz, translated from French, which was itself translated from Russian, comes back to its author after a journey of five long years. He is struggling to remember his phrasing, just as you struggle to recognise long lost cousins, but there is no possible doubt: it is his work.

At the end of the reading, everyone is agitated. They consider all the possibilities. Is it an impostor? How long before he gets arrested?

"I bet it's a Western journalist, actually," someone brags. "You can tell from his expressions, like 'mystical moustache' when he's talking about Stalin. You'd never catch one of our writers saying anything like that. He'd have to have an unbelievable sense of inner freedom."

"I don't buy that," an old silverback says. "Believe me, I've seen it all. It's by one of ours. Otherwise they wouldn't have made such a fuss about it. All that carry-on, reading out extracts... It's so that we can be prepared. Methinks the appropriate services have already sussed him out. It won't be long before they... snap!"

At this rather unappealing prospect, Abram Tertz bids his comrades farewell, affecting an indifferent attitude. Stay neutral, immobile, as dull as a wall! On his way home, he nearly breaks into a run.

That night, he sleeps poorly.

He's not the only one.

Lieutenant Ivanov is summoned urgently back to the office for an unexpected call-out.

"Duty mustn't wait," he says soberly to Larissa.

A peck on his wife's cheek and hop! he's down at the front of his building, where a car is already waiting for him, with Sergeant Gladkov at the wheel.

"What's up?"

"You need to stand in for Grishkin. He was on call tonight at the office, at the eighth directorate, but then he was summoned for an emergency by the commander of the ninth."

A most unusual procedure, to say the least. The order must have come from very high up.

"Grishkin has been sent to the ninth?"

It's no wonder he's surprised, in fact. The ninth is an elite directorate which looks after the security of members of the government. You have to be athletic (Grishkin drinks too much), have twenty-twenty vision (Grishkin wears glasses) and extensive general knowledge, so you can be a good conversationalist (Grishkin does not like books).

"Yes, but he's the only one of us who knows how to sew," Gladkov says. "He's so quick! Have you ever seen him mend something? With his big hands? It's unbelievable."

So Lieutenant Grishkin has been mobilised to the ninth, in the middle of the night, because he can sew.

It's absurd.

And yet General Zakharov, the commander of the ninth, called him in person to confirm that precise point.

"I'm told you can sew."

"Affirmative, General Zakharov, Sir," Grishkin said.

"Well then, get your arse over here immediately. It's a matter of State importance. Bring a needle and thread, and your balls. We're waiting for you at the mausoleum, on Red Square."

"What colour thread, General Zakharov? How thick? To sew what?"

"Your cock!" Zakharov barks.

He's on edge. Grishkin makes haste.

Red Square is not empty.

The entire perimeter is blocked off. They're rehearsing the October Revolution parade for November 7, Grishkin realises.

But in fact, not at all.

It looks as if that is what is happening, but it's just a smokescreen. The heart of the square is protected from view by high wooden panels. Grishkin passes the control point and approaches the mausoleum. What is all this commotion?

Soldiers perched on ladders are unfurling a long white banner saying "LENIN" and fixing it to the black marble above the entrance.

There seems to be something missing.

Where's the other guy? Where is "STALIN"…? Since 1953, we had all got used to the fact that they were both there in the mausoleum, lying side by side for the rest of eternity. Lenin, Stalin. Stalin, Lenin. You can't have one without the other.

Grishkin is shown down into the tomb. A side staircase leads to the chemistry lab. There, on a table, under bright lights, he sees an open sarcophagus. It's Stalin. He is right there, sleeping peacefully, not a bit disturbed by all this light, embalmed by the best specialists in the world, those who did Lenin. A unique procedure. Alchemy! His complexion breathes. His moustache is in tiptop form. There's a kind of tension in his face.

Hey, what if he isn't asleep? What if he's actually secretly observing us?

It's absurd, but it looks as if his eyelids don't quite meet. Maybe he's only pretending to have his eyes shut, like you do when you're cheating at blind man's buff, spying on everyone. Best not to look… Keep your head down.

Grishkin notices that he is not the only one looking the other way.

Two guards take hold of the body and move Stalin into an ordinary coffin, made of wood covered with black cloth. The box is a little too narrow, they have to push down on his shoulders to pack him in.

"Do you have everything you need to do the sewing?" they ask Grishkin.

"Affirmative."

"Well then, let's go."

The commander of the mausoleum advances, white as a shroud. He makes quick work of it. He unpins the star of the Hero of Socialist Labour decorating Stalin's chest, then, pulling out a pocketknife, cuts off all the gold buttons from the uniform.

He's got the willies too, Grishkin guesses. What if Grandpa Stalin grabs him by the arm?

When he's done, the commander hands a box to Grishkin.

Inside are five brass buttons.

"Hurry up and sew them all on properly."

Grishkin has never moved so fast.

All around him, crushed by the enormity of the task, in front of a Stalin who could still bite, no-one is breathing a word.

Once the new buttons are in place, they shut the coffin at last.

"Nails… Where are the nails?"

We forgot the nails in the rush!

We absolutely cannot leave the door of death ajar.

So the commander himself trots off to the workers in Red Square, brings back some nails, and bang! bang! bang! bang!

That's it. That's the worst of it over and done with.

Six men then carry the coffin to the Kremlin wall, where a grave has been dug.

He'll feel the cold, Grishkin thinks.

No more cosy mausoleum for him!

Later on, Grishkin finds out that Stalin's exile is the

result of a decision taken the previous day, at the Party's Twenty-Second Congress. That old Bolshevik witch Dora Lazurkina, a member of the Party since 1902, in other words since the Pliocene, made a speech, her voice wavering with *vibrato*:

"Our wonderful Vladimir Ilyich, the most human man there ever was, cannot rest in eternal peace next to the man who... Comrades! I carry Ilyich forever in my heart, and that's why I survived, comrades, even in the most difficult moments, because I had Ilyich beside me and guiding me. Yesterday, I asked Ilyich for advice, as if he were right there before me, in flesh and blood. And he said: 'It is abhorrent for me to be next to Stalin, who caused so much misfortune to the Party.'"

Eighteen years in the Gulag, her husband executed in 1938 – it does leave a mark.

Lazurkina falls silent, and a wall of applause springs up. Khrushchev leaps to his feet:

"Exactly!"

Everyone is suddenly standing up. Bravo!

The mystical moustache is sentenced to move house.

It's a delicate operation, touching on the sacred. General Zakharov comes to direct operations himself.

"I want two big concrete slabs directly over the coffin."

Just to be sure that the Ogre does not rise up again, one moonless night, to go back and sleep at Lenin's again.

The commander, shaking all over, has some reservations:

"The concrete might squash the coffin like a pancake. And Comrade Stalin's body along with it."

Zakharov reflects on the matter. Does he really want to be recorded in the annals as the one who took upon himself the responsibility of destroying the saintly relic?

"Look at these poofters!" the general sneers. "The guy's been dead for eight years, and they're still pissing their pants with fright."

Finally, he gives in. Courage also has its limits. Otherwise he wouldn't be a general.

We'll do without the concrete slabs.

A thin marble plaque is placed over the tomb: "J.V. Stalin – 1879–1953"

Just a little mound, nothing more. No statue, no flowers, no bust.

When he gets home, Lieutenant Grishkin's nerves are shattered, and he cannot resist opening one of the little white bottles from his reserve.

He drinks alone, in the dark, repeating the day's enigma to himself: where have Comrade Stalin's gold buttons gone?

The next morning, at the time when children set off for school, Abram Tertz is awoken by kids screaming in the street under his window:

"They turfed Stalin out of the mausoleum! He got chucked out! The stiff's gone walkabout!"

The panicked adults intervene at once:

"What do you think you're up to with this stupid game? Shut your traps! If someone hears you! You have no idea! Break it up right now and keep your gobs shut!"

The astounding news is confirmed during the course of the day. Abram Tertz cannot believe his ears. Nor can Lieutenant Ivanov. There's no way to go and check either, Red Square is still blocked off.

Both of them are rather pleased with the news.

"He deserved a manure pit," thinks the one. "But that's a good start."

"You have to know how to move on," thinks the other. "The Party is always right."

X

"Larissa, we've got trouble at work, really shit trouble."

Half a glance is all it takes for Larissa to be reassured. The really shit trouble does not concern them directly.

"Watch your language, Evgeny. And let me remind you for the umpteenth time that you're not supposed to talk about your job, even to me."

"Well, that's the thing. I need to," Ivanov insists. "You have that sensible objective viewpoint. It's about Lieutenant Grishkin. He's hit the bottle."

Larissa shrugs: show me one single adult Russian who doesn't have a problem with alcohol. On that score, she hit the jackpot with Evgeny: never a drop too much, not even at New Year.

"He's been drinking, and it's getting worse. Ever since he touched Stalin's body. It's like a slippery slope. He came in to the office unshaven – he had forgotten we were having an inspection! Nikonovich saved his bacon by stopping him in the corridor and tidying him up with his razor. And his breath! We gave him pickle juice to drink."

"Great idea, pickle juice," Larissa says. "There's nothing quite like it to get over a hangover. And to polish metal. And it's good for sunburn too."

"So here's the problem: the way he's going, Grishkin will end up like Captain Tropinin, but even worse off."

Tropinin – a legend.

At pistol practice, during assessment sessions in one-handed shooting, when the arm is extended, Tropinin was a catastrophe. Shaking like an old rag. But only if he had an empty stomach. If he'd had a drink in the preceding half hour, it was the exact opposite, he would be transfigured into a crack shot. An incredible interpenetration of dependence on alcohol and the physical capacity for concentration. Knowing his weak point, Tropinin carried a hip flask wherever he went. Like a diabetic with insulin. How did this escape the eagle eyes of his superiors? It's a mystery.

Despite being repeatedly dobbed in and searched without notice by the inspectors, he was never caught *in flagrante* with alcohol on his person.

And he never smelled of it either. As if his throat had the ability to recycle those guilty vapours.

He killed himself by falling into a lift shaft.

Annoyed at having to wait for a lift that was taking too long, Tropinin smashed the metal door – he was built like a tractor – and having poorly anticipated the resistance of the panel, hurled himself into the void.

A good comrade, that Tropinin. Always happy to pull his weight. Never opposed to doing something slightly stupid. Not frightened of anything. Sometimes violent with the suspect. Old school. And the jokes he used to tell! Tropinin's famous jokes…

"Grishkin is not the first boozer in Russia, and he won't be the last," is Larissa's analysis of the situation.

"Yes, but he's an immoral boozer. He's cheating on his wife now."

With an informant, no less.

Aurora Borealis is a woman of easy virtue – that's why she was recruited. All of Moscow's depraved intelligentsia have had a go with her. A mine of information, is our Aurora Borealis! And also an excellent means of putting pressure on men, who sometimes become more cooperative post-coitum, especially if they're otherwise married.

Ivanov had always wanted to have a Mata-Hari in his stable. Now he's wondering whether he didn't have a far too romantic view of his profession.

Of course it was never his intention to sow discord in Grishkin's domestic life. He had even warned him: "Watch out for Aurora Borealis, she jumps on anything that moves." Grishkin, who was investigating the trade in blue jeans at the school of medicine, didn't want to hear anything about it.

Infidelity is contrary to the Soviet ideal. The real communist does not betray his wife: not only is it dishonest, but it also saps your vital energy and occupies your mind, which should be dedicated entirely to the success of the Revolution.

Grishkin has erred, has doubly erred, as a man, and as an officer of an elite corps.

It is now Ivanov's duty to have a conversation with his comrade. To set him on the right path again. But ladies first. Grishkin will get his turn after Aurora Borealis:

"What got into you?" Ivanov fumes when they meet at the usual place for her monthly update.

Aurora Borealis sticks a papirosa into her cigarette

holder. A wide belt with a huge matching buckle accentuates her splendid waist. Her blond hair is piled on top of her head in a sophisticated patisserie creation.

"I don't see what the problem is. I sleep with whoever I want to. We love each other, me and Kolya."

"That's impossible," Ivanov protests. "Lieutenant Grishkin is married. His wife's name is Elena."

They sit facing this fact in silence for a while.

Aurora Borealis lets out a little snigger:

"You can be such a reactionary sometimes! Faithfulness, you say. Virtue. The sanctity of the family… Blah blah blah. Your attitude to love is just so retrograde. Would you want the priest to make a house call before you have sex every time? You do know that Lenin had a mistress, as well as his wife Nadezhda Krupskaya, right?"

She doesn't even lower her voice to expound this blasphemous postulate.

"Why do you think Inessa Armand was given the honour of being buried in the Kremlin wall? With a State funeral? She and Lenin – you know what I mean…?"

Ivanov senses something close to mockery.

To associate the sainted name of Lenin with debauchery, and thereby justify her own repugnant behaviour! Does this woman not know what she's risking?

"You'll have to get used to it, Comrade Ivanov, feminism is for real. Remember the words of Alexandra Kollontai, that woman who helped us rid ourselves of bourgeois prejudice in matters of possessive love: 'Refusing the traditional family structure will liberate women from disagreeable domestic work, create the conditions for their professional development, and contribute to the formation of collective consciousness.' Would you dare contradict Alexandra Kollontai?"

What a fearsome creature.

I'll never hire another woman as an informant, Ivanov resolves.

"Don't you go breaking up the Grishkins' marriage," he says simply. "Or there will be consequences."

He pronounces that last sentence with icy firmness, so that the snake can feel the danger in the ocean's undercurrents.

"There's no way I'm gonna break up anything. They haven't fucked for months."

There's quite a contrast between this woman's refined beauty and her language, which is way over the speed limit.

He has to save Grishkin's skin somehow.

"You should report this to Colonel Volkov," Larissa decides.

Ivanov takes one for the team.

Sometimes being a mate, a responsible mate, means figuring out what the most appropriate external pressure is.

Ivanov describes the situation.

He doesn't snitch about the alcohol.

Colonel Volkov has undeniable human qualities. And he's quite the strategist! His analysis is crystal clear:

"When Vladimir Ilyich was blocked in Tsarist Russia, he emigrated: that's called circumventing an obstacle. Once the conditions for the Revolution were in place, he came back in top form. We'll do the same for Grishkin. Take another path. Keep him away from the forbidden fruit."

What is wrong with all these people, citing Lenin to deal with that miserable Grishkin?

A temporary mission order is immediately issued.

The blue jeans business has become a national sport, so Grishkin is sent off to the provinces, a thousand miles from Moscow, to one of the regional hubs.

"Six months at Novocherkassk will do him a world of good. He can pull himself together."

"What about his missus?" Ivanov worries. "Aurora Borealis was emphatic: they're not having sex anymore."

It's Larissa who finds the solution again:

"Let's invite them over for dinner, for a meal between colleagues. I'll have a talk about it to Elena. Woman to woman."

Zero alcohol served.

For dessert, fruit salad.

The day before, by a stroke of luck, Larissa came across some Brazilian oranges being sold on Dzerzhinsky Square from huge boxes with multi-coloured labels. Thirty minutes or so standing in the queue, and her string shopping bag was filled with two kilos of sunshine to take home – the maximum being sold per person so that there was enough for everyone, in other words until midday.

People stopped her in the street: "Where did you get them from?"

A con man even tried to buy them off her for double the price, on the pretext of a marriage banquet.

Larissa did not fall for it.

The day of the dinner, she sliced up the oranges and some apples, in a ratio of one orange to five apples. A tablespoonful of Georgian cognac. Some raisins soaking at the bottom of the bowl. A little powdered sugar.

As for the apples, it was Ivanov who had found some,

a month ago, at Voentorg, of perfect quality – from Poland!

For appetisers, a salad of beetroot, potatoes, cabbage, and tinned peas, seasoned with sunflower oil. Tinned fish in tomato sauce. Potato and onion salad.

"Wow, this is quite the spread!" Grishkin whistles, his eyes roaming over the table in search of a bottle – in vain.

"We only drink tea at home," Larissa warns him immediately.

Is it any surprise that Grishkin remains rather taciturn?

Ivanov asks him questions about his work at the moment, the blue jeans. This is the top priority project. It's a powder trail, an epidemic. Some people would sell an eye to get hold of a pair.

"It's their brains they've long since flogged off," Ivanov sneers.

Grishkin agrees. Two hundred roubles for a pair of jeans? Can they not see how totally obscene that is? A pair of trousers is still just a pair of trousers.

The fact is that there is no shortage of trousers: everyone has a pair. Show me a man walking down the street with no trousers! And if that's the case, then why do they have to be blue jeans? It's simply ridiculous.

Ivanov remembers how he and his mates used to hunt down the guys in their zoot suits, when he was a young member of the Komsomol. Those degenerates infested Gorky Street, which they called "Broadway". You'd see one, with his trousers dyed red or platforms stuck to his shoes, back him up against a wall, and do a nice snip-snip job with a pair of scissors. Then call him "Tulip" – because of the shreds of fabric that looked like falling petals. What sissies! Those pipsqueaks would spend a fortune on Western-style clothes, and then cry like girls in their hacked-up outfits, begging, offering money...

One moron, he still remembers, struck a sardonic martyr's pose while they were cutting up his tight-fitting trousers with a razor, then started reciting something that almost sounded like poetry: "The schlubs are out in their thick skins, take pity on the schlubs." Then, directly in Ivanov's face: "Aye-aye, Sir schlub! Little schlub, schlubik, schlubushka, schlubette, schlubly, schlbuchik, schlubocrat."

They did not beat him up – members of the Komsomol do not behave like brutes – but it wasn't because they didn't want to.

What is wrong with all these people, trying to make themselves stand out from the crowd? What is it that makes those zoot suit guys or that Abram Tertz think they are above the common lot?

Grishkin then explains how he dismantles the blue jeans networks.

First of all, there are jeans and jeans.

There are real jeans: Levi's, Wrangler, or Lee, if you want a pedigree. Mustang is not so good. But still impossible to find. Much cheaper, much much cheaper are Bulgarian jeans, with no defined brand. Not easy to get hold of either.

The real scourge is the counterfeit jeans. To identify them, you need to rub them with a wet matchstick: if the blue comes off on the tip, they're fake. They're made from hessian taken from old postal sacks marinated for twenty-four hours in a bathtub with a bottleful of blue ink.

When he's conducting a house search, the bathroom is the first place Grishkin pokes his nose into.

"The blue ink gets into the scratches. It looks like veins under the enamel."

Meanwhile, in the kitchen, over a casserole dish of noodles sprinkled with cheese that she is browning off in the oven, Larissa has her little talk with Elena.

It just goes to show, you have to put out for your husband. That's our lot, for us unfortunate women, whether we like it or not. With men it's a physiological thing – the seed needs to get out sometimes! Otherwise, watch out for the boomerang effect! It's not an impossible task, once a week, after all. He'll be reassured in his self-esteem, do better at work, be more committed, it's good for your relationship. And if you don't want children, don't rely on the man to pull out. You can work out when you're ovulating. But there's another method, apparently, although you have to proceed with caution. An elderly neighbour from when we were still living in our old communal apartment told me about it. Apparently you have to think about frightening pictures from fairy tales ("What big teeth you have, Grandmama!") during the act, or just beforehand, and that will make children run away, and therefore prevent fertilisation. Larissa doesn't think much of it though. In any case she's actually trying to have children at the moment, so she thinks more about pictures of happy princesses or defeated dragons – but with no results so far.

Faced with all this science, Elena is sceptical. Having children? That's really not the issue.

And it's not that she's not willing, it's just that Grishkin isn't up to much lately. His mind is elsewhere. And his drinking isn't making things any easier.

One night, she tried to touch his… thinking that would stimulate him.

"With your hand?" Larissa asks incredulously.

What a depraved idea!

"It's not that I was keen, I just wanted to do the right thing. A childhood friend of mine, who's a little crazy sometimes, bragged that she had done it. So I thought I should give it a try."

She should not have. Grishkin leaped out of bed and called her a whore. "How dare you? You, the mother of my children!" He was beside himself.

In other words, you have to wait for it to happen naturally.

For the miracle to happen, Larissa suggests, there's a remedy that might help. Her husband isn't exactly a horn-dog either, with all his worries about work and his responsibility for the country, so she uses a scientific mixture, Spermocrine, produced according to the method of the eminent chemist Kravkov from bulls' testicles. She got hold of some vials from a pre-war stockpile: Zoya, a friend from uni, who now works at the central laboratory of Michurinsk, has let her have some at mates' rates. Ten drops here, ten drops there, in the evening meal. He'll never even know it's there.

Elena goes home with the witch's brew.

The following week Grishkin is at Novocherkassk.

They will never see each other again.

Years later, Ivanov will find his trace in the archives.

XI

The events at Novocherkassk in June 1962 shake up the Competent Authority, and eventually have an indirect impact on the fate of Abram Tertz.

The madness starts on the first of the month. In the shops with their chronic shortages, the prices for meat, butter and milk leap by 30 per cent.

The same day, the workers of the locomotive factory at Novocherkassk learn that the production standards they must achieve in order to get their pay packets have also gone up by 30 per cent.

It's like a double curse.

A spontaneous gathering assembles in front of the gates of the manager's office.

The factory manager loses his temper: "If you can't afford to buy meat, go stuff yourselves with offal pirozhki." Marie-Antoinette could not have put it better herself. Kurochkin, his name was, the manager's. Kurochkin, which means "of the little chicken".

Whether it hit the mark or not, the ill-fated spark nevertheless sets the powder keg of history alight.

A message scrawled in chalk springs up in the corridor: "Hail the working class! Khrushchev to the knacker's yard!"

An impatient finger sounds the siren.

That's it, the electricity is cut off. It's a workers' strike – in the country of triumphant socialism! The factory grinds to a halt, the workers walk out and block all the trains at the nearby railway station. There are five thousand of them. The police try to push the crowd back, a fight breaks out, three policemen are assaulted.

That evening the situation deteriorates. We should cut off the gas supplies to all the factories in the region, a striker suggests. Occupy the post office! Cut the telegraph wires! Send out a call to the whole country so the revolt spreads!

Faced with all this, the Competent Authority is mobilised – but completely overwhelmed.

Anything lying around gets requisitioned: Grishkin's team is called out as a matter of urgency to evacuate the managerial staff holed up in the factory. Kurochkin is extracted disguised as a worker, wearing a safety helmet and blue overalls.

Khrushchev is notified. The Minister of Defence, Marshal Malinovsky, a keen photographer and chess player, issues a few orders.

That night, tanks and troops are brought in.

They occupy the strategic points of the city: the bank, the post office, the police stations, the town hall.

Early the next morning, things start heating up. A crowd gathers on the main square, then starts to throw stones.

A few factory workers climb up onto the town hall balcony, wave the Soviet flag, and brandish Lenin's portrait, all the while demanding salary increases.

They think that Lenin is with them, that he is protecting

them. What an odd reflex, running under Vladimir Ilyich's petticoats whenever you get a little boo-boo.

Down below, there's pushing and shoving and shouting. One cry rises above all the others: "Down with the police!"

And the insults fly! And the spittle splatters! An empty bottle of vodka takes flight. It hits a soldier's honker.

Frightened, the fifty or so guards in front of the town hall, armed with machine guns, fire in the air.

"They're shooting blanks!" someone shouts.

Like hell they are!

Second warning.

A kid who had climbed up a tree to get a better view of the spectacle smashes to the ground with a perforated lung.

Nobody notices him.

One worker recognises the smell of gunpowder, strong and bitter, just like when he was in the army.

"They're actually shooting, the fuckers!"

Too late.

"Fire!"

*** *** ***

Twenty-five corpses. Thirty or so wounded.

The people finally understand what's going on. You should have seen them run! Panic stations. As if in a gust of wind, the square is empty! Shoes left behind, a shopping bag, newspapers, caps, glasses, hair curlers.

The clean-up starts immediately. Like a disagreement you want to forget as quickly as possible.

Grishkin and his team have their work cut out.

Other strong arms arrive from Rostov.

Look lively!

The bodies are evacuated and buried in several cemeteries around the region. The families are kept away. When they ask for information, they are told: "You're not to know, not to know, not to know." Or shouted at: "You should have kept a better eye on your son!" A reflex: isolate them from each other. No-one is allowed to communicate with anyone.

Nothing happened at Novocherkassk on June 2, 1962. It was hot – a lovely sunny day. Your husband has disappeared? Don't worry, the authorities have the situation under control. Did your husband like to drink? Was he ever violent? No wonder he got into trouble. Some people just love to sow discord and drag everyone else down with them.

It was an accident, a horrible accident.

Who told you shots were fired? What's their name?

The injured are gathered together at the hospital, where they are given a stern telling-off, one by one: this is what happens when you let provocateurs infiltrate good people. All that blood, it's your fault! You should have been more vigilant and morally staunch enough to resist provocation. You won't build the future by protesting like idiots.

Others are told: yes, there were shots. Some hooligans tried to take a soldier's weapon, the others responded.

Another explanation: it was the protestors themselves, through the voice of their representatives, who shouted "Fire!" Yes, absolutely! Why would they do that? It's obvious: they didn't want any dodgy individuals, no doubt in the pockets of foreign powers, to take hold of the movement for the purposes of anti-Soviet propaganda.

So no-one really knows exactly what happened.

The square in front of the town hall is cleaned with a

fire hose and scrubbing brushes. The soldiers get lumped with the job. They messed up, they clean up. That evening, inspection from the high command: the blood is gone, but there are still bullet holes.

"Pave the whole lot over!"

A polishing machine is brought out. The statue of Lenin and the facades are covered in pock marks from the bullets. Scaffolding goes up to hide them. They get plastered over and repainted.

It's not every day you see builders working so fast. They're really going for it!

The town is under curfew. Whispers circulate that Novocherkassk will be razed, like Carthage. If they were prepared to shoot into the crowd with machine guns…!

The evening of the incident, the arrests begin – more than two hundred of them. What a job!

You take people away in the middle of the night, just like in the good old days. You identify the ring leaders.

The diseased organ is isolated: there are roadblocks set up around the town, and the railway station is closed.

New public health measures are put in place: it is forbidden to walk in the street or to gather in groups of more than three people.

For fear that some amateur radio buff tries to be funny and send information to the outside world (or abroad!), powerful jamming stations are brought in and set up around the town.

Once the new tarmac is down, a festive evening is organised on the very spot where the blood flowed – nothing happened, we're telling you. Dance!

Without quibbling about their hours, officers of the

Competent Authority hold a private conversation with every single inhabitant who saw anything at all. The nurses at the hospital, the hairdressers in the salon across from the town hall, the kids who were up in the trees.

And, of course, with the soldiers and policemen.

Who are forced to sign the following document:

"I, such and such, soldier in the so and so regiment, hereby certify that I am committed to fulfilling the governmental mission which I have been assigned. Once this mission is carried out, I undertake to keep all its circumstances secret. If I should betray this State secret, I would be subject to the highest possible sentence: the death penalty."

The surviving factory workers have learnt their lesson. By the following Saturday, the production standards are significantly overshot. They're working like champions now! People are even falling over themselves to do volunteer work, on Sundays, to compensate for the three days that the factory was shut down.

One month later, there's a show trial: seven guys are condemned to death. The charge: "Attempted *coup d'état* against the Soviet state."

One hundred and five others are given hefty labour camp sentences.

The finger that pushed the siren button at the factory: ten years in the Gulag.

The artist who made the placard with "Meat! Butter! Higher salaries!": twelve years in the Gulag.

The clever guy who took down Khrushchev's portrait from the factory facade: ten years in the Gulag.

A young idealist, Nikolai Stepanov, nineteen years old,

dares to ask the judge: "Your honour, who gave the soldiers the right to use weapons against a peaceful group of demonstrators?" Fifteen years in the Gulag for that legal genius.

Otherwise, nothing happened in June 1962 at Novocherkassk.

In fact, if you asked any of the inhabitants five or ten years later, they would all unanimously say: "What a lovely month of June that was, such beautiful weather, I do remember that!"

The factory workers would frown: "No, I don't remember anything. But we got a bonus in December. And a bottle of cognac for New Year."

But Grishkin would never say a thing.

As soon as the factory is brought under control, he drowns himself in the Tuzlov River, in a state of advanced inebriation.

For Grishkin, there were too many emotions to process, too many traces to disguise.

That man was cracked inside.

Enough to make you wonder whether he did actually belong to the big family.

But let us not forget that he was not the only one who was shaken by the events.

Something like an electric shock hits the Competent Authority, which didn't see it coming. A popular uprising in the home of socialism, how is that even possible…? The lack of respect… "Khrushchev to the knacker's yard!" Who put that freedom into their heads? Where are the safety rails, the moral compass…? It's all very worrying.

Some of the high-perched officers get insomnia.

Is everything falling apart in this country subjected to relentless Western propaganda?

No, we can't just resign ourselves to this!

Our elders, who led the glorious Revolution and made so many sacrifices, do not deserve this!

Arise, ye guardians of workers' rights!

The fragile neurons of Novocherkassk have no doubt been debilitated by anti-Soviet discourse that we must identify and exterminate.

Action stations, quick smart!

While the summer thunderstorms wash the statue of Lenin in the town centre, the Criminal Code is unbolted and bolted back together again, tacking on Article 70, which will become the alpha and omega of this ideological shield. It targets "acts of propaganda conducted with the purpose of undermining or weakening the power of the Soviet Union", "the distribution to the same ends of calumnious fabrications that discredit the Soviet state and its social system", as well as any person who creates or possesses subversive material of this nature.

Anyone caught in the jaws of Article 70 sees their life collapse: the expected penalty can be up to seven years in a labour camp. The reach of this new bronze sword is wider than the old Article 58-10, and its limits less defined. The drag net for criminals is thus more manageable, and the fishing zones it can cover are more extensive.

Abram Tertz does not read the Criminal Code – he does not want to do his head in. Mrs Tertz, on the other hand, gets hold of a copy, as per to the old adage "don't let your enemies take you unaware". She reads it at night to help her get to sleep.

Just as Lieutenant Ivanov and Investigator Pakhmonov do.

Each of them wonders where to find the letter and how it will be applied.

And thus, on both sides of the law, the robber and the policeman toss and turn in their beds.

Goodnight, sleep tight!

XII

Monocle likes to go out into the countryside for picnics, to get up to a bit of mischief and feel alive. He and his friends go and spend a few days in a big ramshackle wooden shed. The timetable includes long walks along the River Oka, homemade rotgut tastings with the local yokels (the famous samogon), water duties (it has to be drawn from the well in tin buckets), forbidden poetry readings (Pasternak, Tsvetaeva, Mandelstam), and great bonfires where they burn anything they find lying around.

Gleb has brought tinned fish in tomato sauce, which he miraculously procured, thanks to his brother-in-law, who filched it from the Crimean fish factory where he works as an accountant. *Sultanka* and *verkhogliad* are the names of the two vertebrates they are readying themselves to eat – no-one has ever heard of them.

The tins get passed around, examined, no-one dares open them.

On the labels, a *verkhogliad* observes them all, with its little eyes on the top of its head, whereas the *sultanka*'s eyes are as big as saucers soaked in vodka.

Finally they finally open the tins.

The smell isn't awful, but it's not great either.

Oh well, you need something to wash down with the drink.

Gleb makes himself an unconvincing open sandwich with lots of pickled cabbage.

The big potatoes, with their occasional blue splotches, are starting to boil.

In the evening, while they're devouring all this, Tolik plugs in a radio, sets up the antenna.

That's why they came here, in fact.

In town, you can't hear anything because of the jamming. Huge transmitters are deployed all over Moscow, hurling out noise over all the frequencies in use.

In the countryside, it's different. You can breathe.

They turn the big button, looking for the short waves.

They only get hubbub and radio soup. Bzzz! Brrr!

"You need to get the radio up higher," one expert suggests.

"And get it away from the stove, especially."

"They've changed the frequency."

"No, it's the unsettled weather that's ruining it, with that low pressure system."

There! They have it. They hear the notes of the introductory music, then a woman's voice, in Russian:

"This is Radio Liberty. Our programming continues."

Everyone is suddenly quiet, as if they were at a Philharmonia concert in Moscow.

But in the background, you can still hear the jamming. Like a swarm of planes constantly flying overhead.

"We are about to read a piece of writing that was published in *The Reporter* magazine, a new story from the U.S.S.R.," the lady says. "You'll see, it's something special."

Then a man's voice, poised and distant, as on the official Soviet radio, announces:

"Moscow speaking. We will now broadcast a Decree of the Supreme Soviet of the Union of Soviet Socialist Republics. In view of the growing prosperity and to meet the wishes of the wide masses of workers, it is decreed that Sunday, August 10, 1960 is declared Public Murder Day."[*]

A bit of *sultanka* escapes from Monocle's gaping mouth. Well, what do you know!

Public Murder Day – Monocle has heard of it, oh yes he has!

Public Murder Day – that was Monocle's idea! It had come to him a while ago now. He remembers: he was at a party, they were being idiots and having a laugh inventing all kinds of implausible commemorative days. In the Soviet calendar, there was a Border Guard's Day (May 28), a Day of the Inventor and Rationaliser (the last Saturday in June), and a whole bunch of other ones, all more or less incongruous. So Monocle burst out with: "And why not a Public Murder Day?"

"On that day, all citizens of the Soviet Union, who have reached the age of sixteen, are given the right to exterminate any other citizen with the exception of all persons mentioned in the first paragraph of the annexe to this decree."

Gleb starts laughing nervously.

"Shshsh!" he is told, with hands, eyes and feet.

"Annexe: Paragraph 1. It is forbidden to kill (a) children under sixteen, (b) persons wearing the uniform of the armed forces of the militia, and (c) transport workers on duty.

---

[*] "This is Moscow Speaking" (trans. Stuart Hood et al., Collins & Harvill, 1968).

Paragraph 2. Murders committed before or after the above-mentioned period, and murders committed in the course of robbery or rape, will be regarded as crimes and punished according to existing laws."

The rest is in the same vein. It's bizarre, dark, and profoundly disturbing, especially since the language used is that of official jargon, peppered with stock phrases.

A parody! What incredible impudence!

The woman's voice takes over again:

"You have just heard an extract of the short story 'This is Moscow Speaking', by Nikolai Arzhak. We remind you that Abram Tertz and Nikolai Arzhak are the pseudonyms of two Soviet writers, representatives of a literary genre that is forbidden in the Soviet Union: fantastic realism."

They listen to the international news: the death of Marilyn Monroe, the failed attack on General de Gaulle at Petit-Clamart, the death of Peter Fechter, eighteen years old, gunned down as he was attempting to escape over the Berlin Wall, not far from Checkpoint Charlie.

Nobody around the table knows who Marilyn Monroe is.

Tolik, a reporter with *Soviet Screen*, has heard the name, but never seen any of her films.

He almost feels ashamed of this, does Tolik.

Then the wind changes, the clouds scud overhead, and it's over, they can't pick up anything anymore. Radio Liberty is extinguished by the noise.

Nothing makes a difference, not even the rather hazardous operation of connecting the aerial to the lightning rod.

Since there's nothing to say about Marilyn Monroe, and de Gaulle is not especially interesting, the conversation lingers on Berlin and its famous wall, which everyone understands to be in the same category as jamming the airwaves: a fight lost in advance, material proof of the ideological failure of the system that is incapable of resisting capitalist propaganda by the force of its arguments alone.

Monocle isn't really joining in.

He could throw in a few provocative prompts, but what's the point?

He realises, with some annoyance, that there is nobody here in this gathering to entrap. All these people are small fry: *verkhogliads* of mediocre existential value, cumbersome *sultankas*. Look at Tolik, trying to show off by boasting that he knows someone whose uncle knows someone who was able to see "Some Like It Hot" during a trip to Belgium. Look at Irina, who remembers another programme on Radio Liberty (or was it Voice of America?) when Abram Tertz was mentioned.

"Has anyone read anything by Abram Tertz?" she asks timidly.

Monocle pricks up his ears.

No, nobody has.

Tertz, Arzhak, those guys have class.

I could have been Arzhak, Monocle thinks suddenly.

What a coincidence, after all, that idea of the Public Murder Day!

Unless it's not a coincidence.

Arzhak must have been within earshot when Monocle had his amazing idea, heard it all, and used it as inspiration.

A good idea, an original idea, a nice and dark one too.

Anti-Soviet too, since it's now being broadcast over enemy airwaves.

He didn't care, did he, that Arzhak? He took Monocle's idea without asking for permission, and now he's being handed the laurels by Radio Liberty and Irina.

"The thing is, that was my idea, Public Murder Day," Monocle says all of a sudden.

Stupefaction all round.

"You're Arzhak?" Irina asks in a little bird's voice.

There is incredulity in her eyes. And some admiration too.

For a moment, Monocle wonders how to play this. He wouldn't actually mind usurping someone else's glory – except that it would be dangerous.

"No, no, it's not me," he says regretfully. "But I was the one who came up with the idea."

He tells them how they played at inventing absurd commemorative days. It was in 1957 or '58…

"But then, that means you know him, you know Arzhak!" Gleb exclaims.

Everybody suddenly falls silent, as if pinned down by the same thought: all it would take would be for one of them to knock on the right door, and Monocle would be summoned, interrogated, maybe even accused of complicity.

Monocle arrives at the same conclusion.

And also: yes, he does know Arzhak. Or, to be more accurate, Arzhak knows him.

All he has to do is remember. Who was there at that party?

Come on now, concentrate.

It was the architects' group, he thinks. Lots of people there. At Professor Lebedev's place. Unless it was at the art history department… Or both. Yes, both. Because, come to think of it, he had thought his Public Murder Day was so fab that he had spread it around in all the ecosystems he had been visiting at the time. People would open their eyes wide, blush, burst out laughing, or flee. It was an ideal provocation!

Don't tell me that he, the born manipulator, the very cunning informant, was in the same room as Arzhak, and didn't understand (he didn't understand!) that he was within reach of a gangster who would soon have a price on his head.

Think, for goodness' sake!

Or let's work by elimination.

It was in Moscow. Of that he can be certain.

He thinks about contacting the Competent Authority, but instantly rejects the idea. What will Lieutenant Ivanov say when he finds out that Monocle was the origin of the degenerate idea that Radio Liberty is now making such a meal of? It's tricky.

Feeling ill at ease, Gleb, Tolik and Irina change the subject.

But it is beyond a doubt that Monocle's aura is now more palpable.

Tolik tops up his glass more quickly.

Irina, at the end of the evening, lets him know that she finds his impudent sense of humour quite attractive. Monocle doesn't forget that he is married (he even has a son) but this pre-flirtation is not altogether disagreeable.

"Try to remember," Irina insists the next morning. "Who do you think Arzhak is? We could encourage him, support him financially…"

The prospect of this illicit knowledge seems to be a real turn-on for her.

If Monocle was Arzhak, she would throw herself at him immediately, it seems.

He is disgusted.

Especially since he simply can't remember.

He makes mental lists of potential suspects, considers them all.

The problem is that he knows too many people.

I'll have to cast my nets again, he resolves. Proceed with subtle provocations and cross-referencing. First the architects, yes. And then the art historians. I'll start tomorrow.

Tolik, for his part, takes the information gleaned on Radio Liberty to the editorial committee of *Soviet Screen*, where he mentions that they could take the same angle on Marilyn's death as their colleagues at *L'Humanité*: it was Hollywood and its capitalist system that killed her.

Well done: he is given a column, in the "News of World Cinema" section.

"The people in Marilyn's inner circle did not help her," Tolik writes. "That's why her nerves could not handle such an uneven battle. The actress was overpowered by the cruel capitalist laws of the film industry."

To illustrate the article, they cut out a black and white photograph from an issue of *Cinémonde*, the French weekly preciously archived in the ed-in-chief's filing cupboard. It gets retouched to make her lips less glossy, to erase her beauty spot, soften the contours of her face.

For years to come, that modest report will be the only thing written about Marilyn Monroe in the U.S.S.R. Tolik will not be so modest as to refrain from boasting about this.

The article in question, while brief, does not go

unnoticed: women of course find the actress vulgar ("those open lips! those half-closed eyes!") while at the same time wondering what kind of false eyelashes she wears that are so long and elegant. The Soviet false eyelashes you can sometimes find in the shops look like exploded car tyres.

As for her hairstyle, some devilish women start to imitate it.

The Marilyn style, however, is less popular than the so-called "Babette" style, a kind of nonchalant beehive that looks as if it was catapulted onto the top of your head with a cocktail shaker. Its incredible architectural audacity is revealed to the ladies of Moscow by Brigitte Bardot in "Babette Goes to War" – which becomes a cult film from one day to the next.

Larissa is curious about it and drags her husband along, whose little red I.D. card lets them jump the queue. They come out of the cinema feeling irritated, as much by the depraved attitude of the heroine as by her impudent tone, that insolent *je-ne-sais-quoi* that seems to make their compatriots swoon away.

"There's no way I'm going to set up a construction like that on the top of my head!" Larissa declares.

But she does swap indispensable tips with her friends about how to manage the *tour de force* – apparently Bardot slicks down her locks of hair with saliva.

Meanwhile, Ivanov, in common with all his office comrades, is busy trying to imitate Yul Brunner's cocky gait from "The Magnificent Seven", the season's other box office hit. An informal competition is organised. Kulakov wins. To achieve that inimitable rolling of the buttocks, he stuck a five-kopeck piece up near his bullet hole.

The performance is a good laugh that contributes to the staff's *esprit de corps*.

Then all the tomfoolery stops. Colonel Volkov, having somehow got wind of it, deemed the exercise morally suspect and unworthy of the Competent Authority.

"You look like worms after a rain shower when you wiggle your butts like that. Leave all that nonsense to those Hollywood degenerates and start setting a good example instead!"

His wholesome anger sets his feckless troops back on the straight and narrow.

XIII

A letter received by the eighth directorate suddenly requires urgent attention. It's a complaint from a French tourist, one Pierre Soupirault, a communist from the Isère region visiting Moscow as part of a tour group. The fine fellow was outraged by what he saw in the capital, and did not fail to inform the management of Intourist, who passed his letter up the hierarchy.

"It started even on the bus from the airport," Soupirault writes. "The driver stopped for a moment and a well-dressed young man in a suit came aboard. He quickly explained to us in French and English that we could exchange our currency for roubles at a much more advantageous rate than with the official bank. He was very friendly and polite. A few members of the delegation let themselves be tempted. He proceeded to exchange the money rapidly, then alighted during the journey into the city.

"The same scene took place at the hotel, as we were waiting for our room keys. A young woman discreetly offered to exchange our French Francs. As I expressed my surprise at this way of doing things, so contrary to civic duty in the harm it causes to the Soviet state and therefore to all its citizens, she replied that everyone did it, that it was part of the order of things.

"Later on, after the visit to the Mausoleum, the Intourist guide took my group down to the riverbank across from the Kremlin. There, in the space of an hour, we were accosted no fewer than twenty times, and I'm not exaggerating. When it wasn't chewing gum we were being asked for, it was clothing (and never mind the size). Marie Trouard, from the Grenoble Section, received an offer to buy her make-up bag (when she hardly even wears any!). She was also asked for French magazines, like *Marie-Claire*, and even ballpoint pens or batteries! The guide spent all her time shooing these pests away, and I must stress that her firmness was worthy of the highest praise.

"What a deplorable image these young people give of the country! It looks as if the Soviet Union has shortages of everything. But especially, it makes one think that the population is basely attached to the most derisory material goods, while the greatest human adventure History has ever known is being played out, that of the emancipation of the oppressed classes. No, really, this was a great disappointment."

Ivanov launches an investigation. Such a missive demands the most thorough follow-up.

Pierre Soupirault, a card-carrying member of the French Communist Party since 1953, was not lying.

Svetlana, the Intourist guide, confirms the account of his misadventures point by point. Indeed in her confidential report on the visit, supplied to the Competent Authority at the end of her mission, she noted that Soupirault tried to have a conversation with her about the street traders. He seemed seriously upset.

Because she was not on duty on the day of their arrival, she cannot confirm the incident in the bus.

However, she draws our attention to a man named Fournier, who, in contrast to Soupirault, did not hesitate to engage the young people on the riverbank in conversation, and even to sell them a book, which, most probably, *he brought from France with the sole purpose of selling it.*

Which book? Ivanov wonders.

Svetlana cannot answer that question.

And now that she thinks about it, she's not even sure it was a book.

Fournier had prepared his deal well in advance. He had taken care to wrap whatever it was in newspaper. When Svetlana asked him about it later (scolding him nicely for encouraging the speculators' uncivil behaviour on the riverbank), he denied everything – all evidence to the contrary! He categorically refused to tell her what book changed hands.

"You should have been a bit more persuasive. How big was the package? What shape?"

It wasn't like a shoe box or something floppy, like maybe clothes. More like a square, actually.

"Singles!" Ivanov realises.

The files show that this is not the first time that Fournier has come to the Soviet Union.

Instead of changing foreign currency, he brings in a few records by Gilbert Bécaud, which he discreetly supplies to strangers on the Sophia Embankment.

No need to make an appointment. He puts his hand up to his ear like a conch shell, leans back a bit, shudders, and is accosted at once. Those starving Bécaud fans can sniff out their favourite treat.

"I don't understand." Svetlana sighs. "Usually the French

are among the most obedient ones. It's the English who think they can do anything they like. They're the ones you have to keep an eye on. But the French! Louis Aragon, Paul Éluard!"

It's enough to make you wonder whether the influence of Aragon and Éluard carries enough weight against the perversions of the capitalist system.

And Bécaud isn't even the worst of it. There's jazz – which is nothing but noise. And then there's this new perversion, which must have come directly from a baboon's brain connected to a 127-volt outlet, known as "rock 'n roll".

You can't even dance to it properly.

In fact all those capitalist dances are just obscene wriggling. You'd think they were invented on purpose to make the popular classes forget the oppression they suffer, through the unleashing of their copulatory needs.

Fortunately, there is Soupirault.

We'll pass on a favourable assessment to the Grenoble Section. If ever Soupirault should feel ready to take on a position of responsibility within the Party, his application would be viewed with favour.

"Except that he's thick as a brick," Svetlana objects. "He wants everything, straight away. He absolutely cannot understand that Communism is in a consolidation phase which will only be completed in twenty years' time. His criticism is not constructive."

What a pain in the arse he is, that Soupirault.

Because of him, we'll have to go on rodent control as a matter of urgency.

A team of covert operatives is deployed on each of the airport shuttles.

To begin with, no results.

The drivers are obviously in on it.

Finally a few arrests are made. Losers with no networks. Aborted embryos of the late Rokotov. Nothing to worry about.

Other operatives disguised as foreigners amble along the Sophia Embankment, with mixed results there as well. The dealers have a sixth sense, it seems. They don't take the bait. You clearly need more than a pair of jeans to pass as a Westerner, Ivanov realises. Foreigners have something that cannot be imitated. A way of walking, of holding a door, of looking at a woman. An aura. An unfalsifiable watermark.

It's a bottomless well: as soon as you catch one dealer, two others take his place.

The Competent Authority does not have the resources to infiltrate everything, to keep everyone under surveillance.

And so you bring in the *druzhinniki* to the rescue. These students from physical education or paramilitary training courses volunteer to use their muscles to preach the word, and get rid of the weeds.

Easy now, no touching foreigners.

But you can give the speculators a good going-over.

Armed with virtuous sadism, the *druzhinniki* burn the chewing gum, smash the lipsticks, snap the records, empty the bottles of perfume, slash the jackets with razor blades.

Sometimes fists caress ribs.

And at the end of the day, the fists unclench, the fingers stretch out and reach for a pen to write a weekly report to the authorities. How many records were smashed, how many jeans ripped?

When the reports reach the Competent Authority, there's so much more work to do!

France is obviously a cesspit. Lieutenant Ivanov holds a book with a creamy white cover: *Fantastic Stories* by Abram Tertz, published in Paris by Instytut Literacki, the Polish literary institute.

The text is in Russian. In Russian! The book is targeted at émigrés, but not only at them. Various institutions make it their business to offer copies to any Soviets authorised to travel to the West – and some morally unstable citizens cannot resist the temptation.

That's the case of Dimitri Maltsev, a professor of mathematics at Moscow University, all greying hair, scoliosis and panicky eyes.

He sits shaking before Investigator Pakhmonov.

"We have nothing against you personally," Pakhmonov reassures him. "You're just the emerged part of the iceberg. Easy to spot, and pointing to the presence of hidden destructive forces. You're doing us a favour, so to speak."

From the look on Professor Maltsev's face, you wouldn't be so sure: there's no trace of pride at having been caught red-handed.

He is accused of accepting the treacherous book, then of bringing it into the territory of the Soviet Union.

"I had no idea what it was," Maltsev ventures. "You know, literature for me… In Copenhagen, at the end of a lecture about the topology of compact spaces, you don't expect… I thought…"

"What are you talking about?" Pakhmonov smiles. "You were very clever about it. You slipped away from your monitor on the pretext of having forgotten your scarf in the cloakroom. That's where you took the book being handed out by a provocateur (we have witness statements to that effect) and you hid it in the pocket of your jacket. Without saying a word to the monitor. While he is bending over backwards, travelling with you, precisely to protect you from such provocations! Anyway, let's move on. Later, when you were questioned by the guard at the border station in Brest, you certified that you had nothing to declare."

"How could I have known? It looked a perfectly ordinary book."

"Of course it did. That's why you spent your time reading it on the sly in the train toilets, and you kindly offered it to your colleague Vladimir Lipschutz... By the way, he confessed to everything, Lipschutz did. We have his statement here."

Pakhmonov strokes a file on his desk.

Professor Maltsev feels as if there are icy fingers grasping his ankle and pulling him downwards, into a lake where he has no choice but to drown.

"You see, we know everything. More than everything, in fact. Our birdwatchers have had their sights on you for a while now. It wasn't enough for you to bring an anti-Soviet book into the territory, you also passed it around to all your friends who are as spiritually defective as you are, so that they could also taste the forbidden fruit. In legal terms, that's called dissemination. An aggravating factor. You've heard of Article 70? I have the list of your friends here, with their statements. Paradoxically – and don't take this the wrong way – you've done us a favour, as I was saying: we had no idea that you maths whizzes were so vulnerable. With all that intellectual rigour we assumed you had! 'The derivative of an exponential function is also an exponential function.' You see, I haven't forgotten all my maths… We're going to have to set this all straight."

You let him stew a little longer. Describe Article 70 and its consequences. The first thing to do, in the short term, is to cancel his trip to Zurich, which he's been planning for two years.

What you don't tell him, however, is that the Competent Authority is hesitating.

What's the point of grinding down an ageing prof? It's not a huge crime, he won't do time for it anyway. Especially since he has friends at the Academy of Sciences. He could be put out to pasture in early retirement. He could also keep his teaching position, on condition that he becomes an informant. Whereas the chemistry department is well covered, it just so happens that we don't have enough eyes and ears in the mathematics department.

"Go on, go home. We'll be in touch again. Ivanov, take this guy under your wing. See what you can do with him."

Extending your network is good, but catching Abram Tertz would be better.

The Competent Authority can only look on in dismay at the increasing distribution of his work. And in Russian now!

Which means: any ordinary Soviet citizen can read it.

Can you imagine the danger?

Lieutenant Ivanov holds his nose and dives into the forbidden book himself.

The stories are odious, indeed. One of them is about a soothsayer who is capable of seeing the past and the future in a kind of total omniscience (but is incapable of foreseeing the advent of Communism). In another one, the hero is a mediocre writer, a monstrous graphomaniac, obsessed by the pathological production of his writing, which appears to be unstoppable.

Not a single positive character: all of them appear puny, bitter, grotesque. No reference to the industrial or agricultural challenges to which the country must rise. No faith in progress, be it social or scientific. And hideous communal apartments everywhere, with leaky plumbing. What Tertz stirs up and concocts is repulsive, deformed, false. No, this is not the Soviet Union in which the lieutenant lives!

Ivanov is not, of course, an expert in literature – each to their own – but, confronted by these horrible stories, he doesn't need to be!

The criminal must be arrested before he writes anything else.

Before he metastasises.

XIV

The terrifying mystery of this cancer is that it has come forth from ourselves. There is no cancer bacteria except in our own entrails, and it isn't contagious except when we look at ourselves in the mirror. Scientists say it is *endogenous*. Suddenly our insides let go of the wheel.

Lieutenant Ivanov knows what cancer is, better than many doctors.

For sometimes a perfectly healthy Soviet citizen becomes a pathogen.

Despite the tons of vitamins we are given prophylactically from our earliest youth. All those Marxism–Leninism lessons. All that antiseptic censorship, which is there for our own good.

Oleg Penkovsky is one of those pathogens.

Penkovsky is the greatest shame of the Competent Authority, and simultaneously our greatest pride.

In this spring of 1963, Penkovsky is the person everyone is talking about – without actually saying anything of course, because the details of the operation are top secret.

Someone told me… Apparently the story is…

Colonel Oleg Vladimirovich Penkovsky, an employee of the G.R.U., the army's spy agency, betrayed the trust of the working class by delivering hundreds of documents about Soviet rockets to the British.

The fact that most of these documents were obsolete or unreliable (as were the Russian ballistic navigation systems) is neither here nor there.

He revealed the command circuits. The precise organisation of the artillery systems. He gave them the names of a myriad of Soviet agents residing in the West.

When he had been decorated twice with the Order of the Red Banner, and made a knight of the Order of Alexander Nevsky!

A year and a half previously, we foolishly sent Penkovsky on a mission to London. As soon as he arrives, he contacts M.I.6. to offer his services. His new friends baptise him "Alex" and furnish him with a miniature camera: the famed Minox model B, with its aluminium casing. Penkovsky delightedly takes its measurements: its length is no more than three matchsticks set end to end.

His motivation remains a mystery. The man has everything: a high double salary, a two-bedroom apartment, the opportunity to travel abroad, medals covering his chest.

It's cancer, so it is!

He spends his time shooting his Minox at all the documents he can lay his hands on, starting with military magazines that are easily available in libraries.

Each microfilm is rolled into a cylinder, which Penkovsky hides in the packets of little chocolate bars. His favourites are Little Squirrel and Northern Teddy Bear. The advantage of this stratagem is that you can (almost) always find chocolate in the shops – the tangible result of the military support the U.S.S.R. gives to various African countries, who settle their debts in cocoa beans.

He delivers his work to Janet Chisholm, the wife of a British diplomat posted to Moscow. They meet in places agreed in advance. Not a word is spoken. Hardly a glance exchanged. The contact only takes a fraction of a second.

Janet takes her baby out for walks in a pram – the ideal receptacle into which to slip a little package without attracting attention.

Of course she knows she is always tailed by an operations team as soon as she leaves the embassy. All notable foreigners are. It's the A.B.C. of a Moscow posting.

Let us not forget that our surveillance methods are the best in the world.

It sounds boastful, but when it's the unalloyed truth, there's no need to blush, you have to say so.

Lieutenant Ivanov fondly remembers his training at K-Prep.

"Train yourselves to do two things at once, and to do them perfectly," their instructor would say, the formidable Major Kobel, nicknamed "the chameleon dog". "Follow the target AND choose a book in a bookshop. Join a queue for bananas AND follow the target. If you don't know which book you're looking for, if you're just hanging around in the bookshop, you'll be unmasked. If you don't know how much money you have left for your bananas, you'll be unmasked. You must constantly be playing the role."

He would also say:

"A passer-by is not just passing by. Each passer-by, and I mean each and every one of them, walks with an elastic band in their head pulling them towards their goal. X is going to see his dying mother in hospital, Y is late for her oral exam, Z is meeting his mate Petya to play chess. If you follow the target without having an elastic band in your own head too, you'll be found out."

At the beginners' level, the practical exercises consisted of picking a random pedestrian at a train station and observing them continuously for six hours.

Then you would get together in groups of three, and practice observing each other or slipping a tail. Twenty, thirty times in a row.

You played cat and mouse and cat. Each student drew the name of another student at random, which only he knew, and had the assignment of observing them for a day. You had to tail your target without being detected and simultaneously keep an eye out for anyone tailing you (of which you could never be sure) – all that for a whole month.

There was also the "eyes in the back of the head" technique: tailing someone while staying constantly *in front* of them in the street, without turning around at every step and without losing your target.

Even harder: "eyes in the exhaust pipe". A variation on eyes in the back of the head, but in a car, where everything goes much faster.

"To shake off a tail, forget about the trick of leaving the train at the last moment just as the doors are closing," Kobel would say. "If you do that, you have a good chance of shaking off a beginner, but you instantly show your hand: first of all, everyone knows that you're on active duty, and second, that you're heading for a meeting. If the bedbugs sticking to your arse are pros, there will always be one on the platform when the other one is on the train. So you shake off the one on the train, but the one on the platform will follow you, and call for reinforcements."

The students, full of admiration, used to say: "Kobel deserves the Nobel."

If the Soviet education system can be proud of one thing, it's surveillance techniques, taught with passion by pedagogical champions.

Janet Chisholm was thus well escorted.

Oleg Penkovsky was no halfwit either.

He chose their live drop points with the care of a chemist handling explosive material.

There was a railway station concourse. Difficult to spot a possible contact in the middle of all those people running in every direction. Once, Penkovsky placed himself just behind her at a queue at the ticket office. Another time, he was right beside her on an escalator crammed with people.

The park where Janet took her baby out for some fresh air, pushing the pram for hours (to exhaust her tail), was the site of a rather conventional exchange: she came and sat on a bench where he was reading *Pravda*. He left at once, but forgot his gloves – chosen in the same grey as the bench so that they wouldn't be noticed from a distance. You can't use chocolate all of the time.

There was also the stocking trick. Having bought sweets herself, Janet realises in the middle of the street that her stocking has come unhooked. Bother, how embarrassing! It's not very comfortable to keep walking while pressing the stocking to her thigh through her dress! To fix things up, she hides in the hallway of the first building she comes to – impossible to follow her in. Once the stocking is adjusted (and the sweets exchanged), she comes out again. A little later, Penkovsky leaves the building.

But all that was not counting on Olga, a young miss from the escort services. Olga is particularly gifted. Did her feminine intuition whisper that there was something fishy going on with those stockings coming unstuck all of a sudden, or was it her extreme perfectionism that prompted her to keep the building under observation for longer than planned?

Whatever the case, she signals her colleagues to continue tailing Janet – she'll catch them up.

And when Penkovsky finally comes out, she takes his photograph with the Ajax 12 set into her coat.

More than that: she starts tailing this unidentified man. On her own initiative! And that could earn her a severe reprimand: she is supposed to be on Chisholm.

So she follows Penkovsky, who isn't at all worried by that student in front of him, over there on the other side of the street, who appears to be hurrying to a date.

Look how she takes her time plastering on more lipstick.

And now she's fussing with her hair in her reflection in a shop window.

"Eyes in the back of the head" impeccably executed!

Penkovsky's exclusively military career has limited his technical sensitivity to surveillance. He did not go through K-Prep, nor did he have the opportunity to perfect his training with Kobel.

The damsel goes into a shoe shop and comes out at once – behind Penkovsky this time. She has changed her hairstyle, put glasses on, and turned her coat inside out. She looks ten years older than her age.

You'd think she was a shop assistant going home after a

long day shouting: "Size 43 is no longer available. There's only 39 left!"

The fish has no way of knowing he is being trawled.

Olga, meanwhile, is surprised to see Penkovsky enter a building of the G.R.U. headquarters.

She doesn't understand straight away. She imagines the G.R.U. has also put a team on Janet Chisholm. A brilliant tactician in surveillance, Olga is a rather pathetic analyst.

Unsettled, she reports everything she saw to her bosses, who don't take long to identify Penkovsky. Given the size of the sturgeon, the best operatives are set on the case.

The rest is a question of operational technique.

We organise for him to be absent by sending him for a medical examination, and search his apartment while he's out. We find his Minox, some rolls of film, a radio transmitter, encryption codes. And an authentic epaulette from the British army, for the rank of colonel.

"Еби твою мать!"

Ivanov, who never swears, can't help himself when this top secret information reaches his ears.

"Vulgar swear words morally demean those who use them," his grandfather used to say, and young Evgeny took this precept to heart.

How can you expect the words хуй, пизда, ебать or блядь to issue forth from the throat of a real communist without his choking on them?

Which just goes to show how appalled he is.

And with good reason, clearly.

When he was passing through London, Penkovsky asked if he could try on a British army officer's uniform – one of his childhood fantasies. He paraded around dressed up to the nines, all handsome and cocky, in front of his hotel room mirror and his indulgent hosts. As a souvenir of that dazzling moment, he kept an epaulette, which he had no qualms about bringing back to the Soviet Union and hiding in a box under a strip of parquet flooring.

You can just imagine the traitor taking it out from time to time, to kiss it like a relic.

It did not bring him luck. Penkovsky is sentenced to death.

Which doesn't stop the account of the final phase of his stake-out from making the rounds.

Penkovsky lived in a building on the riverbank, and apparently a cable several hundred metres long was laid from the building opposite on the other side of the Moskva River, where an operations team was watching his apartment through a telescope. That's how we controlled a spy camera mounted on the balcony of the apartment above his. The cable ran down the facade, hidden in the wall, then across the riverbed, where it was fixed by divers.

A technical exploit.

It is essential not to exaggerate – the facts are already incredible enough.

They say that when he was arrested, Penkovsky started blubbering like a little girl. And also that he proposed a crooked deal: he would continue to pretend to work for M.I.6., and use that as a way of passing false information to the British. The authorities pretended to agree to this, just to make the traitor cooperate, and then sentenced him to death anyway. Who did he think he was fooling?

XV

With the regularity of drops of water plopping onto the forehead of an unfortunate torture subject, Abram Tertz is relentlessly spoiling the mood of the Competent Authority. Every three months or so, a new translation pops out, bearing witness to the international dissemination of his work. Japan, the Netherlands, France.

Here's a new one. The Plon publishing house has just brought out a three-hundred-and-thirty-page anthology, compiled by Jean-Marie Domenach (him again!). It includes the *Fantastic Stories*, "The Trial Begins", and the inescapable *On Socialist Realism*.

The translation is by one Sonia Lescaut. We gather intelligence immediately: she is a journalist with *Arts* magazine. Approached gently on several occasions by our contacts in Paris, she knows nothing, has not the slightest idea of the real identity of Abram Tertz. She worked on the Russian published editions without ever having seen the manuscripts.

At Plon, no-one knows anything either. They're publishing a book without knowing who the author is. You'd never hear of such a thing in the Soviet Union.

Jean-Marie Domenach could be a lot more helpful to

us, but the man openly mocks any attempts to make him come clean. And even boasts about it publicly:

"When I received the first article by Abram Tertz at the end of 1958 – how it got to me, I won't say, for there are people who are far too interested in finding that out – it was one of the greatest joys of my career," he writes in the preface.

He's a tease.

"It was as if the telephone suddenly rang and someone was speaking from the Great Beyond: an interrupted communication miraculously re-established, a free and fresh voice coming from a world that we were no longer receiving any messages from except propaganda and ready-to-wear literature."

"Propaganda," Domenach says, does he? Yes, well, first of all propaganda is not a swear word, when the goal is to build a future society liberated from the capitalist yoke. It's a source of pride, for us idealists.

But this dithyramb is annoying nevertheless.

Ah! we could show him what for, that Domenach, if he should ever turn up in Moscow. We would take tender loving care of him, we would – he's not superhuman is he? He has a weak spot. Everybody has a weak spot. The French, it's a fact, are always in heat, all you have to do is find the right angle, girl or boy, we can do either, and snap! he's caught in the mousetrap.

A honey trap actually, usually reserved for diplomats, military attachés, big whales full of secrets, but we could ask for an exception for Domenach.

Every once in a while, Ivanov loses himself in daydreams. Which manifest themselves as a loss of productivity.

He doesn't read Domenach's preface beyond the first page – you must admit it's hard going when you have to check so many words in the dictionary.

The intern on the staff, a young sergeant called Lyuba, attracted by this book in French, cannot resist the temptation of leafing through it.

Lyuba has just celebrated her twentieth birthday. She was born in Ufa in 1942, in other words on another planet, deep in the misery of the rear guard where the evacuees all piled up, a thousand miles from Moscow. Back home, her mama was an occasional translator to an eminent Frenchman, whom she was also supposed to keep under surveillance, Monsieur Maurice, they used to call him. Maurice Thorez. A deserter from the French army stripped of his citizenship, the leader of the French Communist Party yet remained a man. In that rat hole that was Ufa, where people ate crows and sucked on roots, he had the benefit of extra rations, reserved for the elite of the N.K.V.D., which only added to his charms.

Hence the fondness of Sergeant Lyuba for the language of Balzac, which she learned from her progenitor, *in absentia*, after he had to go back to his newly liberated country as soon as the Germans were expelled and all danger past.

Hence also her devotion to the cause of international proletarian revolution.

An irreplaceable internal motor that heightens her attention to detail.

"Lieutenant Ivanov, have you seen this?" Lyuba asks, bursting into his office with the book in her hand. "That Domenach doesn't know how to hold his tongue!"

And indeed, in the middle of the long preface, the following passage appears:

"What do we know, then, about Abram Tertz? That he is Russian, young, and not called Abram Tertz. But then, why this Jewish-sounding pseudonym? Maybe because he is Jewish, maybe because he isn't. When so many Jews hide behind 'Christian' surnames, is taking such a pseudonym not placing oneself firmly in the camp of uncompromising protest?"

Ivanov and Lyuba translate this passage together to be sure of what it means.

"Abram Tertz is Russian!" Ivanov understands.

The blind spot is suddenly clear.

What dumb fucks we are: Abram Tertz is Russian, of course!

We've been on a false trail for three years.

Yesterday Olga, tailing Penkovsky, today Lyuba: women are decidedly rising again in the lieutenant's esteem.

They run to the investigator.

"Colonel, Colonel, Abram Tertz is Russian!"

The first moment of stupefaction past, Lieutenant-Colonel Pakhmonov breaks into a magnanimous smile.

"Respect to that swine! We thought he was a softy, turns out he's the one leading us by the nose."

There is unfeigned satisfaction in these words – something almost like national pride. Being hoodwinked by a Russian is not so humiliating.

"A Jew would never have the genius idea of trying to pass as a Jew," Pakhmonov declares.

With the Russianness of Abram Tertz now a working hypothesis, the circle of suspects is widened.

One piece of good news brings another. An informant announces that a third-year geology student, one Sasha Vesnik, has been seen in possession of several copies of *Fantastic Stories*, in their Russian edition.

Apparently he even boasted to his friends that, on request, he could get a copy… *signed by the author.*

Ivanov falls off his chair. That's all we need!

Just imagine the criminal signing copies of his book, like a celebrity, in full view of all our honest citizens and competent organs!

A surveillance operation is immediately set up.

You have literally to glue yourself to the young man and take note of the names of all those who penetrate his contaminated circle. His friends, his acquaintances, his contacts, everyone. Then you widen the surveillance to his parents – his father is one of the managers of Mosfilm, the State film studio, so you have to proceed with kid gloves.

After a month, in the absence of anything whatsoever that might be compromising, Sasha is summoned for an interrogation.

Sasha Vesnik is not looking at all comfortable. Mosfilm or no Mosfilm, no-one is above the law.

The strategy remains the same. You apply strong but vague pressure.

"In your opinion, citizen Vesnik, what is the reason for your being summoned here?"

And then you let the guy stew in his bad conscience.

"Come on, Sasha, a brilliant student such as yourself. With such a distinguished papa. It's strange that you should be brought here for an interview. You must know that it's never for nothing."

A bad conscience is like nature, it abhors a vacuum.

And so Sasha finally cracks – wide open, in fact.

"If this is about the film evenings, I've got nothing to do with them, I just used my dad's card."

He collapses in tears.

What film evenings? What is he talking about? Let's listen closely.

It turns out that there have been clandestine projections of foreign films organised in the dusty basements of the geology department.

Above the yellowing fossils stockpiled down there for centuries, the enterprising students unroll a screen. A certain Lev Dodolev, known as Lev-Lev, an engineer in training, sets up a 35-mm projector, a Bauer picked up in Germany in 1945 and cleverly adjusted with all the passion of which only a real cinema buff is capable.

Papa Vesnik's card lets them penetrate into Mosfilm's sacrosanct storage room, where the reels of foreign productions reserved for private projections for high-ranking Party dignitaries are stocked – most of these films have never been shown on Soviet screens, and never will be. You "borrow" a reel on Saturday during the lunch break, and put it back in its box on Sunday. And you don't overdo it: no more than one film per week. And it sometimes happens that Vitya, the lab's old caretaker, has some spare unused film: you butter him up with a present of some kind so that he knocks together a copy for you.

There are whispers that Lev-Lev and his team own a collection of one hundred and fifty films from the West.

Imagination has eyes bigger than its stomach. Only a dozen or so are found during the house searches.

One of them is the latest hit right now, "8½" by Federico Fellini, which won a prize at this year's Moscow International Film Festival.

That crap! Ivanov thinks crossly.

He does not understand. He went and saw it at the Rossiya cinema when it had just come out, using his red card to jump the massive queue waiting patiently before the box office. In the packed cinema, stuck between two ecstatic spectators who appeared to be drinking ambrosia from the screen, he spent the longest two hours of his life – more tedious even than the training sessions for static surveillance they did at K-Prep, when you had to stay hidden in a car for six hours without taking a leak.

He came out with the feeling that there was a giant chasm separating normal people from all those intellectuals swooning at such incomprehensible nonsense.

Luckily normal people are in the great majority. Larissa is normal. Lieutenant-Colonel Pakhmonov is also normal – which doesn't stop him from being a great reader. He always has a classic in hand: Chekhov, Gorky, Tolstoy.

Then there's Kulakov, who is hyper-normal. So normal it's frightening.

But really now, how dare the capitalist press write that freedom in the Soviet Union is only so-so, when that "8½" rubbish is shown to all and sundry, right here in the middle of Moscow? A film that gives those wannabe intellectuals the opportunity to hone their superiority complex, without defending any of Lenin's teachings.

Khrushchev didn't understand a thing about the film either.

After an international jury awarded it the first prize

at the Moscow film festival, there was some trepidation in upper circles: how could you show this film to Soviet citizens, when Mastroianni is so obviously contaminated by bourgeois ideology, and Fellini's so-called art is the very opposite of socialist realism?

Like an altruistic mad scientist, Khrushchev decides to test the poison on himself. A private showing is organised for him. The good fellow falls asleep after twenty minutes. "8½" is deemed to be soporific and inoffensive.

Relief all round: if Number One has come away from the experience unscathed, then ordinary Soviet citizens are not in any danger.

So you grant the authorisation for its distribution.

Then, faced with the success of this incomprehensible film, you have to ask yourself: what do people see in it, that so many of them should line up at the cinema box offices like that?

So, prophylactically, you put a stop to it. The film is taken off the screens. Prevention is better than cure.

From one day to the next, "8½" becomes the film in highest demand for Lev-Lev and his enterprising friends.

A clandestine viewing costs the astronomical sum of twenty roubles. The venue is small and they wish to remain discreet: fifteen seats max. It's best to get a personal referral. And to book your ticket a long time in advance.

It goes without saying that this is "income without labour": unacceptable parasitism, while honest citizens earn an honest living.

This is how hunting a whale can bring in a shark.

The gang is arrested. The geology students are expelled from university. Lev-Lev, as the person responsible and the owner of the Bauer projector that was essential to the whole set-up, gets five years. The old caretaker is lucky: he precipitously retires.

Papa Vesnik's career stops dead. He is transferred to a Mosfilm branch in Leningrad.

As for the whale, we'll have to try again. While Vesnik junior did own a copy of *Fantastic Stories* (only a single copy), he never tried to distribute it, and even less to sell it.

Those promises about the author's signature? He was just showing off, the little bullshitter, as a way to impress the girls at uni.

XVI

Great is the Soviet Union, vast its territories, warm its entrails. This is what Lieutenant Ivanov learns to his cost when he is sent to Uzbekistan for an *ad hoc* mission.

"I hope you'll be back in time for New Year." Larissa sighs.

"Apparently Bukhara is a magnificent city," the lieutenant replies, avoiding the heart of the matter – this time, it really *is* Secret.

His mission consists in analysing the anti-Soviet discourse said to be circulating in Uzbekistan, and to participate in "dismantling those defeatist humours".

"Why Bukhara?" Ivanov asks Colonel Volkov.

"Because."

Something has happened there.

When he arrives on the spot, he is taken by military truck to Pamuk, a village three hours' drive away. In the barracks there, where he is quartered, he sees engineering troops running all over the place and artillerymen on their anti-tank canons. Who are they going to be shooting at?

The soldiery knows that something unusual is going down (you can see it in their tired, worried eyes, their uniforms soaked with sweat and fear), but no-one is talking.

The instructions that this is Secret are being scrupulously respected, Ivanov notes in his report.

Finally he finds out: the desert is burning.

Ten miles away from Pamuk, a gas well has caught fire. And it's not a tiny flicker. A flame seventy metres high, like a gigantic blow torch, rises from the centre. In a fifty-metre radius around it, the desert is burning, literally: little bursts of flame keep popping up from the ground all over the place.

At the barracks there's a block specially reserved for the geologists, who have been rushed in from all over the country.

Ivanov's mission is to keep an eye on all those brainboxes, including the associate minister for mining exploration, and several big knobs from the university.

There are times like these in geology when no stone can be left unturned, he notes with a certain amusement.

Those civilian chatterboxes have looser tongues than the soldiers.

They tell him about the accident:

"Imagine a red-hot knitting needle pricking a hot air balloon."

While drilling through a particularly hard layer, the workers pierced an enormous pocket of compressed methane, mixed with hydrogen sulfide, at a pressure ten times higher than normal. Inappropriate tools: the drill was too soft and the stem too fine. Disregarded guidelines: when you see 300 atmospheres on the manometer, it's time to get busy and put reinforced armature in place.

The drill (which weighs several tons) flies off like a drinking straw. They find it later two hundred metres away.

A gigantic golden geyser attacks the sky. The metallic

structure of the drilling shaft starts to melt and collapses. Pockets of gas near the surface explode and widen the opening. You suddenly feel so small!

"Imagine you're a grain of semolina which falls out of the pan and you're watching the flames on the stove."

Impossible to get anywhere near it because of the heat. And it's not for lack of brave or brainless men – none of the special suits are sufficiently heat-proof, nor any of the tanks.

They try to extinguish it with water, then sand, then soil: you might as well try to extinguish a volcano by spitting on it.

The engineers work out the numbers: the amount of gas burning every day is equivalent to half the consumption of Moscow.

Last solution: blowing the torch out with an explosion. As if it were a candle.

"Without carbonising your balls," the associate minister contributes.

The colonel in command of the barracks, with his military tact, proposes they drown the torch with a hefty aerial bombardment, and that'll be the end of it. A handful of bombardiers would be up for it. The officers approve. You'd have to evacuate everything around it, since you couldn't guarantee the precision of the drop.

A realistic geologist howls in fright and reminds all these sabre-rattlers that you risk enlarging the opening, or even causing a fissure in the pocket, and then…

"We're talking millions of cubic metres of compressed gas here. By comparison, the Tunguska meteorite will look like a pony's fart."

A compromise is struck: they'll carry out an artillery

strike. Ten canons set out in a semi-circle will fire simultaneously, aiming at the mouth of Hell. The deflagration needs to blow out the flame, or at least throw up enough soil to block the hole.

They work through the details. You need razor-like precision, therefore the B-11 anti-tank canons will be used, with their 107-mm calibre. But there's a problem with poor visibility at that distance. The powerful movements of hot air deform the landscape and blur all the vertical lines. And when you get closer than two hundred metres, the damn heat makes the tyres melt. So they bulldoze some mounds together, so that the B-11s can be positioned higher up and have a straighter firing line. The men sweat and swear, profusely, continuously, from all of their pores.

The flood of unmentionable words that rises to Lieutenant Ivanov's ears during this bewildering week pops the cork of all human standards. As if a pocket full of incandescent еби сука бля had just been pierced, causing a geyser that was just as uncontrollable as the initial gas leak. Everybody is on edge.

"Despite their nervousness, the troops are working tirelessly to extinguish the torch at Urta-Bulak," Ivanov writes in his report, putting a positive spin on it. "The village of Pamuk has been placed under curfew, as a precautionary measure against information leaks. The order not to speak to any civilians is being respected by the soldiers. The geologists, strictly confined to barracks for the present, require additional monitoring and regular supervision. The drilling expert A.A. Ramensky, besides having a tendency to drink, appears excessively pessimistic. In the nearest city (Bukhara, 136 km away), nobody seems to be aware of anything. The general population explains the presence of numerous military vehicles as part of planned manoeuvres, which occur frequently in the region. As of December 10, 1963, there are no foreign citizens residing there. It would nevertheless be advisable to place Bukhara under restricted access [forbidden to foreigners] to avoid any risk."

The reports must be faithful to the truth (no hiding or minimising the facts), clear (therefore short, easy to read and understand), impersonal, while also suggesting solutions (for a communist, no situation is inextricable). Any proper names are typed in capital letters, so that they immediately stand out. An army of secretaries copies them into registers on reception, accompanied by the document number. A clever filing system, with multiple references, will assist with later searches – by family name, geographical zone, type of incident, relevant military sector.

Since A.A. Ramensky has never been placed under observation before, there is no trace of this individual in the Competent Authority. He gets what's coming to him: Lieutenant Ivanov's report names him personally in a highly sensitive context, so he is accorded the honour of a personal file, lickety-split.

Meanwhile, three thousand kilometres away from the Erica onto which his biography is being frenetically typed, A.A. Ramensky, in flesh and blood, is present at the artillery strike.

The last adjustments are carried out, then they wait for night to fall. The darkness provides more contrast to the flame and allows for more precision in aiming at the edges of the crater. The sensation of heat is lessened too – it's a psychological thing.

With the black of night all around it, what power there is in that torch, gushing straight out of the bowels of the earth!

But we are not midgets either, with our canons!

Engineers know how to get the upper hand over nature.

Man forged from the alloy of progress with class struggle is capable of reducing a mountain to dust! Need one even mention that he has already defied gravity to explore outer space?

The capitalist chains that bind the hands of the proletariat are so much more solid than a little ignited gas!

"Fire, еби сука бля!"

The sound wave thumps you in the chest.

A cloud of dust, sand and burning soil masks the point of impact for an instant.

The flame wavers in the blast. Then flares up stronger than ever.

It's a complete flop: the strike destroyed the last of the metal structures, the only ones that had not already melted away, because they were off-centre.

"How are we going to lay the cables now?" the defeatist Ramensky laments. "Before, we had an anchoring point, we could at least use a winch. Now with this heat, there's no way we can even approach the surface of the crater."

The next morning, his face is red and puffy and there are bags under his piglet eyes.

"You've been drinking again," Ivanov says.

"Not a drop!" the rogue answers in a huff. "Never on duty. And believe it or not, I couldn't care less about alcohol. Right now for example, I don't even feel like a drink. Try offering me one, you'll see!"

Ivanov does not take him up on this suggestion.

At the first meeting of the morning, when there are decisions to be taken, Ramensky falls asleep in his chair. While the others are taking stock of the failure of the artillery operation and its consequences, the expert geologist is snoozing!

"Aleksei Alexandrovich!" the Colonel roars. "What do we do now?"

He doesn't even stir.

The dean of the University of Sverdlovsk, a city closed to foreigners, famous for its geology faculty, intervenes:

"There are two remaining solutions. Either we drill a tunnel five hundred metres long and attempt to get in as close as possible from underneath. We put a ton of explosives down there, with the aim of provoking a landslide that will block off the gas pocket. The problem is that it will be difficult to dig so close to the leak. And it will be highly dangerous."

"Or?" the Colonel says impatiently.

"Or we dig a shorter tunnel. And let off a nuclear device."

Deathly silence around the table.

"What? What did I say?"

The dean is perfectly at ease with this modern idea. He is surprised at the tense reaction. He is convinced of this: used in civil engineering, the atom will be an invaluable ally for the geologist of the future. He has already talked about this with the minister. This will be a going concern very soon. Extinguishing a gas torch with a nuclear device – as simple as building a bridge! And we won't stop there while we're at it. In his filing boxes he has another grandiose project: reversing the flow of the River Lena over thousands of kilometres. A few clever explosions, and you'll be able to create a sufficient fall between the levels to bring water from Siberia to the deserts of Central Asia. With all the sunshine here, if you add water, imagine the cornucopia of fruit and vegetables you'll harvest! As much fresh produce as you want!

Well, here is someone who isn't wearing black-tinted glasses, that's good to see.

Ivanov does not mention him in his report – optimism is supposed to be the natural component of Soviet society, why should you brag about it?

You don't make progress by gazing in admiration at your own belly button.

Ramensky, on the other hand, gets what's coming to him once again, but reported with objectivity:

"Even though he doesn't say anything overtly anti-Soviet, his tense behaviour creates a fertile ground for the development of a negative, potentially unreliable attitude."

In return, Ivanov receives the classic instruction to "bring Ramensky into line", which means making him think twice about being clever.

They take the same train back to Moscow.

In time to be home for New Year! Won't Larissa be happy!

"You do understand, don't you, Aleksei Alexandrovich, that the tiniest leak from you about the incident in the gas field which you just witnessed will be considered a treasonous act against the State. Which, to be perfectly clear, means: bang! bang!"

He's starting to talk like Shmakov now. While he's at it, Ivanov adds (reluctantly):

"Bang-bang, and confiscation of all your assets. Your children…"

There are times when you do have to use the children.

"Your children, as I was saying, will be deprived of everything and placed in an institution. You have two, don't you? Sergei and Nina, very talented little kids."

You add their first names to sound more convincing.

"You won't be able to say we didn't warn you, that you were not informed."

Ramensky doesn't know where to put himself behind his ghostly pallor.

After the stick, comfort, always:

"We could have had you fired from the university for being an alcoholic. Falling asleep in the middle of a crisis meeting, really now, what a disgrace! Well, you'll be pleased to know we are going to give you a second chance. On the condition that you stop drinking. You're a great scientist, a world-renowned expert, you should know all there is to know about the dangers of alcohol. Come on now, get a grip on yourself! Look how worried we are about you in the highest echelons. I'll drop by to check up on you every week, unannounced. But shh! It will be our little secret."

And to conclude, on the platform, as they are taking their leave:

"Here you are, for New Year. I got you some chocolates for Nina. And a little tin truck for Sergei. You wind it up with a key, look. It's hard to find these, you know. A real Zaporozhstal. It's written on the chassis. Well then, best wishes for the New Year ahead! And go easy on the booze."

We're not monsters, are we?

Do you know many Competent Authorities who give

chocolates and toys as presents? Who fight so hard for the health and moral standing of the population?

I love my job, thinks Ivanov.

And his job loves him too: he gets a few extra days' leave. Just in time for New Year.

Rarely have he and Larissa been so happy.

An individual apartment. A New Year tree. And on the very top, they put a spire with a red star, just like the ones on the towers of the Kremlin.

Larissa gets out her father's glass toys. How fragile they are!

There's the penguin with clips on his feet. Little Red Riding Hood. Father Christmas with slanting eyes. The Little Snow Girl. The gherkin. The squirrel. The tiny bell.

Ivanov has acquired a Sputnik.

"This year I only want glass toys," Larissa declares.

For this aesthetic reason, the papier mâché "Stalin" locomotive, and the big cardboard star stamped with the hammer and sickle have been left in the drawer.

However, a few mandarins are now hanging on the tree.

They are Larissa's pride and joy.

A few days ago, she ran into an old school friend, now married to a railway manager working in the freight department. Hence the tip: a car full of mandarins coming from Georgia will be arriving especially for the holidays at the Kursk railway station. There will surely be a way to come to an arrangement, for a reasonable price, with the deputy signal box manager.

Which is exactly what happened.

Mandarins!

When even Voentorg did not see their colour this year – well, not in the store for subaltern officers anyway.

Larissa also has some tins of Yugoslav green peas – an essential ingredient in "Olivier" salad – bought last July and kept under the bed. The other ingredients are easy to get hold of: potatoes, carrots, eggs, cooked sausage, dill pickles. The mayonnaise that binds together all these chopped up little cubes of joy is always available at Voentorg – and thanks to Ivanov, Larissa's cousins in Orel can also have Olivier salad with their New Year dinner.

There's a "herring under a fur coat" on the table too, as there is every year. Chopped up fine or put through a grinder, the herring hides at the bottom of the salad bowl. It gets covered in a "coat" made of layers of cooked potatoes, carrots, boiled eggs, onion, green apples and beetroot, all soaking in mayonnaise (again).

And here's the star of the show: sparkling wine known as Soviet champagne. Produced by the continuous flow fermentation method, a revolutionary process invented by Professor Agabaliants (winner of the Lenin Prize, 1961), which also includes the addition of sugar syrup in the last phase for a smoother mouth feel. The best champagne in the world!

Larissa takes the crystal flutes out of the sideboard, having rubbed them earlier with a slice of potato for a brilliant sparkle.

Once a year, you're allowed.

Seated around the table are also Shurik, Lyonya, their fiancées and an old general from a border guard regiment, long since retired, whose face was burnt in the war when his T34 tank caught fire.

During the course of the evening, he tells the story three times.

It was through the hatch in the hull of the tank that he escaped. Thanks to his narrow hips, he managed to wriggle out. His mate, whose trousers were one size larger, got stuck.

"It was one of our own mines that blew us up! We move to attack. Suddenly there's a hail of shells. We try to move back into the clearing. Our sappers had mined it behind us!"

Come on, it's nearly midnight! Let's have a toast! And a kiss! 1963 is over: a new year, a new happiness awaits Larissa and Evgeny. Who knows, maybe a child? They both make a silent wish for one, each for the other.

Everywhere in Moscow glasses are clinking.

Abram Tertz and Masha gaze deep into each other's eyes and raise a toast with vodka.

Another year gone.

Another year when he did not get arrested.

They clink glasses again.

"I have a present for you," Masha says.

It's an extremely rare little brochure published in 1908, *The Customs and Songs of Prisoners in Siberia*.

"That way we'll be prepared for when you go there. You love folklore, don't you? Ethnography…"

"It's probably changed a bit in fifty years, I imagine."

"Well then, you'll just have to find out, won't you, my dear."

On the table are herring and gherkins, black bread, and a big cream pie, with five candles on top. It's five years since *On Socialist Realism* was published. And he's still there, is Abram Tertz, drinking vodka and lusting after his wife, all with complete impunity.

It's insane.

Miraculous.

They savour this miracle alone, in perfect solitude. No friends with them. A black spaniel their only witness.

What does 1964 hold for them? Best not to think about it.

They'll get busted sooner or later, that's all they can be sure of.

But that's no excuse to play the martyr in the meantime.

"How about we make a baby?" Abram Tertz says, drunk.

They've thought about it many times without going ahead with it. Foolhardy though they may be in their game with the Competent Authority, they still feel responsible for the tiny being that would emerge from the void into this family with a Damocles' sword hanging from the ceiling in every room.

The future is a huge sea urchin. How can you make a baby when you are living with a suspended labour camp sentence? What kind of life would you be giving the child?

"On the other hand, if we don't do it now, we're going to have a bit of a technical issue once you've been caught," Masha says.

Right then, let's go. Just you wait, 1964, you'll see what we're made of!

XVII

Monocle loves the Manège. This building, in the shape of a big yellow and white brick set down in the centre of Moscow, has the proportions of a mousetrap. Whenever Monocle goes inside it, he feels as if the doors could shut behind him without making a sound, just like the whale's jaws on Jonah, and nobody will ever hear of him again. A delicious shiver. Long ago it was the Tsars' stables, then a barracks, before it became an exhibition hall. Its functional Empire style, all cold, contained power, is in the image of this country, where people can disappear as if they had never existed.

Or is it actually a temple? In that case the high priest might well be called Monocle. He so loves to wander through it with his friends of the day, dazzling them with his paradoxical aesthetic opinions. There's nothing better than the Manège for throwing out mischievous provocations and making a note of reactions.

And indeed, here he is today, wandering around surrounded by a dozen or so potential clients. The exhibition is called "Moscow, Capital of Our Motherland". Two thousand five hundred works, more than a thousand artists from all over the Soviet Union. Painting, sculpture, etchings, etc.

The canvases are overflowing with colour, lots of flowers, blue skies and Stalinist skyscrapers. The children are happy playing ball, the mamas are pushing their prams, young pioneers with dazzling white shirts and bright red scarves are building nesting houses for birdies.

Lots of craftsmanship in the execution. The perspective is always linear, the bodies correctly proportioned. You can tell these are not Sunday painters.

"Two years ago, in this very room, precisely where we are standing, is where the famous avant-garde exhibition was held when Khrushchev blew his fuse," Monocle recalls.

Everybody has heard about it. There was quite a bit of abstract, expressionist stuff, and lots of portraits in "*art brut*".

Khrushchev was annoyed. The forms were beyond him. Why did they have to drag him here? And all those people who looked as if they understood it all, appreciated it. Comments here, analysis there – he was getting worked up about it all by himself. The rustic hothead sensed something like mockery, like unbearable in-crowd snobbery at his expense.

And the steam made him blow his boorish top.

"What are these ugly faces on this canvas here?" Khrushchev growled. "Don't you know how to draw, or what? My grandson draws better than you do! Are you men or pederasts? Do you have a conscience? I say this is all useless crap. This is not what the Soviet people needs. We must pull it all out by the roots."

"Men or pederasts," verbatim. The artists present were given a good chewing out: their art was called "crap", "scribbles", or "turds".

As a result, there is no longer an avant-garde anywhere to be found. Pulled out by the roots indeed.

Monocle points to the canvases around them:

"So here we are again back at square one, with socialist realism."

Boris, an admirer of modernity, rages:

"It's a catastrophe, a kind of brick wall of misunderstanding."

Monocle jumps in.

"Tragic, you're quite right! Falling out with our best talent, to now inherit all this academism… There are more than a thousand artists here – what for? They're all copying each other. It's like watching grass grow. At the Manège, boredom smells of oil paint."

The group blushes with delight. There's so much freedom in this man!

They look like a young miss who has just got her first raunchy love letter, in secret from her mama, thinks Monocle.

And out loud:

"Someone should go ahead and cast off the shackles and write something about socialist realism. Something that would set the record straight about what is actually a form of religiosity. Yes, religiosity, I do not use the term lightly."

Suffer the little children, and forbid them not to come unto me.

That's all it takes to set Boris off, boasting:

"I've already read something rather scathing on that subject."

When the prey is near, try not to move too fast, Monocle thinks.

"Best not to mention it in public," he whispers conspiratorially.

While at the same time drawing a mental diagram. Boris' parents, what do they do? Isn't he the one with an uncle at the Writers' Union? Or is it through his wife? She knows Joseph Brodsky, the poet… She's even on friendly terms with Nadezhda Yakovlevna, Mandelstam's widow, the woman who learned the entirety of her husband's secret works by heart, because she did not trust paper. We are in the highest intellectual spheres here. Is it possible that…

Not far from their group, a fellow in a threadbare suit is observing them.

Monocle has the feeling he's seen him somewhere before. What does he want, that woodlouse?

This is so unpleasant, it almost looks as if he thinks they are old acquaintances.

The man is staring at him wordlessly through his glasses, his back stooped under the exhaustion of the universe.

They wander into another room. Monocle forces himself to appear carefree. Out of the corner of his eye, he can see that the woodlouse has followed them. He does not approach, he is keeping his distance, looking only at Monocle, glowering at him, guzzling him up with his eyes. No gestures, no signs, just a fixed expression and stinging black eyes.

Hang on, hang on – that's not Kabo, is it?

How changed he is!

He's the same age as Monocle, but looks fifteen years older. They haven't seen each other since… since… it must have been 1949.

In 1949, at the age of twenty-four, Vladimir Kabo was

arrested for anti-Soviet activities and sentenced to ten years in a labour camp, at the same time as his mate Yuri Bregel. Monocle should know: he was the one who entrapped them and dobbed them in.

An excellent piece of work, which earned Monocle a voucher for a brand-new bicycle. A German brand. With excellent road handling and a comfortable seat. Lavender-coloured (yes, lavender!).

At the time, standing before the investigator, Kabo was thunderstruck, but the charges had grabbed him by the throat, the information was precise, and first-hand.

"Tell us about this anti-Soviet short story you wrote."

They refresh his memory.

"The one about a soldier in the Soviet army who goes into a house abandoned by a German family. And who, through reading the books on their shelves, establishes a friendship with these Germans he doesn't know. In other words, who fraternises with the cosmopolitan enemy."

That short story, written out in longhand in a school supply notebook, Vladimir Kabo had shown it only to Monocle, that aesthete capable of appreciating art like no-one else.

Monocle had said that it was "profound, human, astral". So good, he had said, that he begged Kabo to let him borrow the notebook. He wanted to copy it out because "we have to preserve the good things before they perish".

A few days after Vladimir's arrest, Monocle visited Mrs Kabo, his mum, who was in a state of collapse, to present his condolences and to ask her, by the way, whether she didn't have any other manuscripts by her son. "He is so gifted, your boy is!" Just to fill out the prosecutor's file.

Kabo and Bregel were also accused of having created a

terrorist cell, under the cover of a literary club, with the aim of overthrowing the government.

The club was Monocle's idea, and he was the one who had insisted on organising regular readings, but he was not among the accused – oddly enough.

A well-deserved lavender bicycle, clearly.

And now he has this pebble in his shoe. Kabo is standing there, in his ragged clothes, and has the brazen impudence to stare at him openly!

He doesn't know it was me, there's no way he could know, Monocle thinks.

The Competent Authority is not in the habit of revealing the names of its informants.

It did not. Kabo had deduced that Monocle had done it by ruminating over every detail of his case. He thought about it every day for all the years he spent cutting wood and lugging shovels full of frozen earth. He identified and followed every little stream, and they all eventually flowed into Monocle.

Kabo and Bregel were released after Stalin's death. They sometimes get together and compare their inner journeys. We were lucky to survive, they think. When should we pay Monocle a little visit?

Easier said than done. Kabo works in Leningrad, Bregel is always stuck somewhere in the provinces, far away from Moscow. You have to organise your life, make up for lost time. There are fiancées to court. University studies to catch up on. What's the point of seeing that turd again? Just to realise, one more time, how naive you had been? The good lord above did not make Stalin kick the bucket just so you could ruminate about the past.

Bregel is a smidgen more vindictive than Kabo. He hangs around the architecture department where Monocle is a student, and isn't disappointed. He sees him twice, once in the library, the other time at the cafeteria. Bregel still has his Gulag haircut: his skull uniformly shaved down to one millimetre of stubble. You can see it from a long way off, like a moon blinking at you. Most of the returnees, still full of shame, wear berets or caps until their hair grows back. Bregel made a point of coming along with his shaved head uncovered.

In the library, Monocle panics, grabs his stuff, and runs away.

At the cafeteria, in front of all his friends, Monocle has the reflex of going to greet his victim as if nothing had happened. Bregel turns away without saying a word or shaking hands.

Since then, no news. The years go by, the wounds heal, and Monocle thinks the affair is forgotten.

Except for a fortuitous university trip that brings Kabo to Moscow, to the Manège.

It's him, thinks Kabo, there's no doubt about it, it's Monocle. He cuts quite the fine figure with his bowtie and his little dandy's moustache.

He's recognised me, Monocle realises. Not only has he recognised me, but also he knows everything.

The ghost follows him silently, through one room then the next, never approaching him or taking his eyes off him.

He's pretending not to see me, the creep, Kabo realises.

Faced with this incandescent glare, Monocle's panache fades. He is not witty or amusing anymore. Suddenly he feels tired, tense and pale.

"All that socialist realism, it's so draining after a while!" the maestro justifies himself.

Leaving his courtiers, he finally turns to this shadow from beyond the grave.

"Ah Volodya, what a nice surprise! I hardly recognised you."

Kabo remains silent.

"What is it you want from me, Volodya? I… You…" Monocle's eyes are livid, his mouth nothing but a slit.

"I don't have time, Volodya. Can't you see I'm busy?"

Fear makes him lose his cool.

"How long are you going to carry on stalking me? You're being ridiculous. Making a spectacle of yourself."

Kabo is no sadist.

He leaves Monocle standing there, in the midst of the paintings of fluttering red flags and sugary pioneers hoeing the sunlit fields.

He disappears.

Monocle thinks he sees Kabo again several times – in the university cloakroom, on the main staircase, even in a car on Kalinin Prospect.

False alarms.

It's not that it keeps him awake at night, but a sense of unease is preventing him from fully enjoying his vocation as an informant.

Just when he had such a promising sucker in that dickhead Boris, Monocle loses his nerve and doesn't follow through. Suddenly he no longer wants to play with his mouse. Heavy exhaustion casts a blight on his life.

How long is this circus going to last? He was nettled by Bregel's apparition ten years ago, with his shaved head, so why should Kabo be returning now? When will they ever stop hounding him?

Since you can never be sure what Kabo might get into his head (and Moscow is small enough that intellectuals are always hanging around in the same places), Monocle decides to take precautionary measures: he talks about it to his wife.

"It was fifteen years ago, I was young, it was under Stalin, I was pressed into it, I was weak, everyone was doing it, snitching on each other, the Competent Authority demanded it. It was either that, or... well I'll let you guess. I'm a different man now. I've matured a lot. I have a family. Lots of friends. An exciting academic career."

"My poor bunny," his wife replies. "Stalinism, thank God, is in the past now. You are a victim, just like everyone else. Come on now, stop thinking about it. Better to concentrate on your doctorate. It's not long now until your viva. Look how proud little Vasily is of you! Vasik, say hello to Daddy!"

With a family like that, you can rest easy. Morale rises, healing progresses. Monocle stops seeing Kabo behind every tree. He goes to the Tretyakov Gallery – no Kabo there either! It looks like the blackguard has finally stopped harassing him. No doubt because he had the right instinct in confronting him, the other day at the Manège. With losers like that, you have to be firm. Not let them gain a psychological advantage.

The nightmares become less frequent. The viva draws near.

Here we are at last, in the lecture hall of the Institute of Cultural History.

Monocle, his throat in a knot, greets the panel of examiners and the audience.

Kruzhkov, the director of the Institute, presents a short biography of Monocle: brilliant articles in prestigious journals, field work in Central Asia…

"Would anyone like to add anything? Are there any questions?"

A little old man stands up at the back of the room.

"I would, Sir."

The wreck comes to the stage, turns to the audience.

Yuri Bregel!

"I would like to read a declaration, written together with my friend Vladimir Kabo, which we think will contribute important information about the candidate's character."

In interstellar silence, he provides all those present with the knowledge Monocle already has.

How they were trapped. Patiently. Deftly. With all the love for a job well done.

And the five years in the Gulag that followed.

"Take a good look at this man," Bregel concludes, pointing directly at Monocle. "This is a stool pigeon of the worst kind. A *seksot*!"

General consternation. Nobody has ever done such a thing, publicly denounced a *seksot*.

Even the word *seksot* is frightening. Nobody pronounces it out loud, for fear it might unleash an occult power. In the lecture hall, young innocents look at each other without understanding: what's a *seksot*? Is it something to do with sex, which seems to be part of the word? Quick whispers bring them up to speed: *seksot, SEKretny SOTrudnik*, a secret collaborator.

Suddenly, everyone understands: they're seeing a *seksot* in broad daylight!

The examiners cannot hide their embarrassment.

Monocle's wife is sobbing.

Monocle, pale as the statue of the Commander, wraps his arms around himself.

Finally, the chairman of the examination panel decides to speak:

"As interesting as this statement may be, I consider that Comrade Bregel is addressing the wrong audience. Here, we are discussing science, and only science."

Another member of the panel takes this further:

"There was an amnesty. Comrades Bregel and Kabo were rehabilitated in 1956. The case is closed. Let us talk about science."

Traumatised, science unclenches its teeth and rises to the lectern. Stunned, with a glassy complexion, it reads out thesis, antithesis, conclusions.

Monocle is awarded his doctorate, with a majority of the examiners' votes.

His viva has gone well, overall.

The chairman congratulates him, with no enthusiasm. The other examiners shake his lifeless hand. They do not linger.

Nobody comes to the planned celebratory drinks. The happy graduate buries himself in his wife's arms.

"I'm done for! My life is fucked. My career is fucked. Bunch of pricks! They only lost five years, whereas I… I…"

Word of the event instantaneously goes round the architecture and archaeology departments, then spreads beyond the university. Monocle becomes a celebrity – nobody talks about anything else. When he gets a little too close: "Heads up, here comes the *seksot*!" His group of friends instantly vanishes. People refuse to shake his hand, everyone turns away from him in the corridors. Those who spent a lot of time hanging out with him, Gleb, Irina, Boris, have insomnia and cold sweats remembering the jokes about the regime they told him. "Fuck, I told him about my D.I.Y. radio to get short-wave broadcasts, didn't I?" "To think that I tried to show off to him, flashing my copy of *Doctor Zhivago*." "How many other people like him are there, working undercover among us?"

You take stock of your friendships, you suddenly become more cautious, you go out less. Your circle of intimate friends tightens. If in doubt, you don't invite them over to your place.

Ivanov also comes to realise that something is not quite right with Monocle: his productivity has tanked.

He misses a liaison meeting.

At the next meeting, he hardly unclenches his jaw.

Ivanov, who has more than one informant in his pocket, soon finds out about the extent of the calamity from his other little birds.

It's a catastrophe: not only has one of his best assets been burnt, but it sets a disastrous precedent for business. For goodness' sake! You just can't behave like that! You don't inform on an informant! Especially in public! Can you imagine the bad publicity! How difficult it will be to recruit anyone now!

The lieutenant is all the more upset that Monocle is under his direct responsibility. If news of the affair should spread round the staff...

Now both of them have long faces, sitting on their bench on Gogol Boulevard.

"Kabo, Bregel – it goes without saying that we will penalise them as best we can," the lieutenant says at last. "We'll keep an eye out for any inappropriate statements, for the least *faux pas*. We're vindictive like that. We give as good as we get."

"Professor Zhitkovsky refused to say hello to me this morning," Monocle groans. "And Glazunov said that he won't co-author my paper on the origins of Samarkand. And all the architects are turning their backs on me."

"Let's allow time to do its work." The lieutenant sighs. "I'll tell you what, how would you like it if we got you a job in another city, at least until the dust settles? We could even send you abroad, for a while. Yes, abroad, my friend. To East Germany. Dresden. Tell that to your good wife, that'll cheer her up."

Knowing how to reward the troops is a good way to develop loyalty.

"But you'll have to pull yourself together, right? Don't forget our projects: Abram Tertz, Arzhak, they're your top priority."

Ivanov had just found out that the West had been enriched with a new work by Abram Tertz, *The Makepeace Experiment*, a novel published in Russian in Washington.

First an essay, then short stories, now a novel! What's next? An opera?

The honour of the Competent Authority is at stake.

That book is one hell of a provocation: it's about a small town in the Soviet Union, Lyubimov, which decides to secede. Despite the activities of a dynamic local Komsomol group and having all the municipal attributes of a normal Soviet town, it declares its independence.

Its independence! The mind boggles!

And if that was not enough, they decide to build a communist utopia, where everyone can eat as much sausage as they want and drink liquor without getting drunk.

Abram Tertz might as well be calling for a *coup d'état*. A grotesque, surrealist one to be sure, but a coup nevertheless. Investigator Pakhmonov's diagnosis is stark:

"Terrorism by means of literature."

Shmakov is in seventh heaven.

"In the good old days… bang! bang! bang!"

In the meantime, the rabbit is still running.

"Come on, old boy, it's time to get mobilised!" Ivanov exclaims on the bench on Gogol Boulevard, and that directive is meant as much for Monocle as it is for himself.

XVIII

At last, we've got him!

Valuable information has just come to hand. A certain Yulian Grigorevich Oksman, a Doctor of Literature and expert on Pushkin, has been caught red-handed. He tried to send a professor at Berkeley, Gleb Struve, a long missive peppered with forbidden poems by Mandelstam, Akhmatova, Gumilyov. Their mule, an American student working on her research in Moscow, was intercepted by the Competent Authority.

Oksman is immediately placed under surveillance.

Then arrested because you need to act fast.

He's an old acquaintance, this Oksman. Arrested in 1936 for "attempting to sabotage the centenary of Pushkin's death by wilfully delaying the publication of the complete works of Pushkin in sixteen volumes, edited by the Academy of Sciences," he was packed off to Kolyma for five years. In 1941, he gets another sentence for "slander of the Soviet magistrates' court", especially concocted for him so that he does not get out too soon. When finally he is released in 1946, he manages to find a position at the University of Saratov. Rehabilitated in 1956. Returns to Moscow in 1958.

Well well, 1958. Just before Abram Tertz's first publication in the West.

Oksman wouldn't be Jewish, by any chance, would he? Looks like he might be.

During the search, we find both meat and drink: a copy of *Fantastic Stories* by Abram Tertz and a copy of *Moscow Speaking* by Nikolai Arzhak.

Given that both these books are impossible to get hold of in the Soviet Union, it's disturbing to find both of them there *at one and the same time*.

Sometimes there are coincidences that are not really coincidences.

He's a literary type too, that Oksman. The kind of guy who would love "8½".

He was apparently seen at Pasternak's funeral, although we have no photographic evidence of this.

He's more than sixty-five, with ten years at Kolyma in his spine, and worn out. He has nothing left to lose. Which would explain his courage: he stands and looks you straight in the eyes, answers with contempt tinted with arrogance, uses his erudition to look down his nose at Pakhmonov. A real Abram Tertz.

We find letters from Struve in his apartment. That agent of American imperialism has written this to Oksman: "I have prepared a document for publication, without any mention of your real name, of course."

"Enlighten me here, would you? That wouldn't be *On Socialist Realism*, would it?" Pakhmonov asks.

"I can't remember," the scoundrel replies. "I'm not a young man anymore. Ten years in the Gulag…"

"Yes, yes, we know," Pakhmonov says irritably.

The interrogations continue. The suspect finally confesses:

"I admit that I received magazines and books from Struve that could be considered anti-Soviet. But I am not Abram Tertz."

Or:

"I admit that I sent unpublished poetry by Mandelstam, Akhmatova and Gumilyov to the United States so that their *oeuvre* could be preserved. They are our greatest poets, and were crushed by Stalinism. Defending their memory is not anti-Soviet. And I am not Abram Tertz."

Stubborn as a mule!

"You published some nasty things in Paris," Pakhmonov reminds him, sure of his facts.

He's thinking about an article that caused quite a stir, "Stalinists Are Still at Large among Soviet Writers and Scientists". A strange title, explicitly vengeful and violent. Signed anonymously, "N.N.", published in August 1963 in the émigré newspaper *La Pensée russe*, and taken up almost everywhere else including on Radio Liberty, it provoked a few panic attacks for the dozen or so snitches it mentioned by name.

Surprise, surprise, one of Oksman's notebooks, seized during the search, contains a draft of the article.

"Come on, now, stop burying your head in the sand," Pakhmonov insists. "You're the one behind this 'N.N.', aren't you?"

"Prove it," Oksman teases. "But make up your mind: if I'm Abram Tertz, as you say I am, why would I sign as 'N.N.'?"

Oksman is serene in his obduracy. His eyes are full of infinite disgust, mingled with the wariness of a scalded cat.

Twenty or so interrogations later, he is released for want of evidence. The Competent Authority could find no witnesses to sustain their case. Apart from Struve's letters and a few jottings in a notebook, his file is empty.

And a judicial error is out of the question.

When a guy is guilty, he gets busted. When he is innocent, he gets released. It's as simple as that.

Ivanov is in raptures about the humanism inherent in the system. You don't want to have your place searched, get arrested, get into trouble? Mind your own beeswax and stop contaminating the ideals of those who want to make the world a better place. No-one is expecting you to be a perfect communist, but at least don't shit on everyone else's efforts. We're not asking you to walk on water, after all! The rules of the game are crystal clear. Nobody is ever taken unawares.

Oksman is expelled from the Institute – it's the least you might expect, given his lack of moral probity. Whatever got into him, to write to an American academic in secret and shamelessly display our dirty laundry? How can you entrust the education of our youth to such a man? That would be entirely inappropriate. He is also excluded from the Soviet Writers' Union. And his name is erased from all editorial committees. This man can no longer have any cultural responsibilities whatsoever. Go on, off you go! Retired.

The disappointment with Oksman casts a pall over the Competent Authority. Are we actually as competent as we claim to be? Never, in living memory of a State intelligence agent, has it ever taken so long to unmask an intellectual.

So a few rustic assassins sometimes slip through the police's net – their crimes are one-offs, circumscribed by the situation at the time. And sometimes clues are erased by chance or there are no witnesses. But Abram Tertz is not in that category. That man is working the long game. There are certainly people who have seen him at it. He undoubtedly read his writing to his wife and friends: Russians who pride themselves on their literary credentials love those gatherings where everyone shares their creative work. Someone took the manuscripts to the West. Someone else published them. That makes a whole crowd of people. And we can't even get off our arses and arrest him!

The soup of disillusion leaves a bitter taste in the Competent Authority's throat. And then, as if that wasn't bad enough, the terrible news breaks: Maurice Thorez is dead.

Just like every summer, Thorez was in the Soviet Union on his holidays, on the Black Sea coast, when suddenly... Sergeant Lyuba is in tears.

The great man's body is returned to France, but his spiritual funeral is held in Moscow.

His name is everywhere, framed in black.

His photograph is everywhere, heavily retouched and printed in big black dots on soggy paper.

Ivanov, like all the officers in the Competent Authority, is supposed to sulk.

French teachers, taken unawares during their summer holidays, already know what the theme of the first few weeks back at school will be: there will be oral presentations on Maurice Thorez, a poster in the school foyer honouring Maurice Thorez, an article about Maurice Thorez in the school newspaper. So you cut clippings from the papers, lay in supplies, just so you don't have to reinvent the wheel!

From *Ogonyok*: "Maurice Thorez forged the French Communist Party, and turned it into a great party, faithful to the principles of Marxism–Leninism." From *Moscow Komsomol*: "The news of the passing of Maurice Thorez has overwhelmed us all. Comrade Maurice Thorez was a passionate fighter for peace."

Ivanov, who also reads *Ogonyok* every week, mulls over the statement by Andrei Voznesenski, the liberal poet adulated by anti-conformist youth (which in no way disqualifies him for short trips to France or Italy): "Thorez loved poetry like no-one else. Sitting past midnight around a table with a simple but generous spread, such as French peasants eat, his son Paul, tall and bright-eyed, recites Paul Verlaine and Victor Hugo. Thorez raises his glass and drinks to poetry."

Faced with such unanimity, the Sophia Embankment, right in the middle of Moscow, cannot contain itself, and suddenly changes its name. All kinds of shady trafficking, foreign currency deals, blue jeans trading and dishonest proposals will henceforth be conducted on the Maurice Thorez Embankment.

Ivanov and all the French speakers are mobilised to clean up the area in anticipation of a visit by a delegation of the French Communist Party.

Some people say that an embankment, a street, a bus station, all that sounds rather ungenerous for such a great man. So it is decided that a whole town should be dedicated to his name. Former Chystiakove, a mining hellhole of 90,000 inhabitants in the Donbass region, hits the jackpot.

Magnificent Chystiakove! Immortal city! Chystiakove is dead, long live Thorez!

The splicing method that served so well for the fashioning of Leningrad was considered – we almost got Thorezgrad! – but in the end we went with the clean and simple option: Thorez.

The first Thorezian is a boy (of course!), born July 16, 1964, at Clinic number 5. He was named Maurice – was there any choice?

At Thorez, under Ivanov's vigilant gaze, a delegation from the French Communist Party pulls the cord on a plaque.

The streets are spotless, water-blasted that very morning at dawn.

The riffraff of Chystiakove have been cleared away – just in time too – by Komsomol volunteers monitored by competent personnel.

Léon Garric, the delegate from the federation of the Hautes-Pyrénées, reminds the audience of a few fundamental points: "The communist parties of the U.S.S.R. and France are united in their views on all current fundamental ideological and political problems. Long live proletarian internationalism!"

Nikonovich cannot help yawning. What's the use of all this verbiage?

Because meanwhile, Abram Tertz is still on the run – galloping in fact!

While he gallops, another illustrious name is framed in black.

One month after Thorez, it's Palmiro Togliatti's turn to die. At Yalta too. After visiting a young pioneers' summer camp – heart attack. For goodness' sake!

Here we go again.

"An intrepid fighter for peace." "A faithful friend of the Soviet Union." "A remarkable leader, not only of the Italian Communist Party, the most powerful in all the West, but also of the international communist movement." "People everywhere are mourning Togliatti, Togliatti the irreplaceable, the progressive French philosopher Jean-Paul Sartre asserts." *Ogonyok, Trud, Moscow Komsomol…*

Just as for Thorez, there's a tidal wave of baptisms. The streets change names like dominoes falling. Bus stations, squares, parks. Even a university, Leningrad's engineering and economics university, pinches itself and wakes up one morning as Togliatti University.

And a city, of course! You can't do less for Togliatti than for Thorez! A big one is chosen, Stavropol. 123,000 inhabitants and factories, factories, factories. Rubber, nitrogen, phosphorus. Togliatti, the city, will be an industrial giant.

Ivanov and Nikonovich are flat out. Since they managed Thorez so well, they get parachuted onto the Togliatti front. Accompanying, supervising, monitoring, clearing.

They've had to swallow so many speeches!

"I'm starting to feel saturated," Nikonovich says.

Ivanov, although he is tired too, takes the opportunity to learn a few rudiments of Italian. *Rivoluzione d'ottobre. Per la pace. Il futuro.*

After every event, you send in your reports. What the atmosphere was like, how clean the streets were. The tone of conversations of the French and Italian delegations, but also of their brothers from Bulgaria, Hungary, East Germany. Were the Intourist interpreters accurate in their reports?

You complete the already hefty files on the foreign delegates. You have to know all there is to know about your allies. Nuances of opinion are just as important as sexual orientation – on that score, Léon Garric, from the Hautes-Pyrénées, comes out of it remarkably well. He seems hetero (he made passes at both his guides) and speedily aligns himself with the merest whisper from Moscow. He has the potential to climb to the top. A shame that the Hautes-Pyrénées federation is such a negligible component of the French communist apparatus – not like Seine-Saint-Denis or the Pas-de-Calais.

The agitation around Thorez and Togliatti has still not subsided in September, thanks to the start of the school year, and even spreads into October: two giant portraits framed in black are to be carried aloft during the traditional military parade to celebrate the anniversary of the Revolution. Thorez and Togliatti are even expected to be placed in front of the usual portraits, those of Khrushchev and…

We interrupt this account for an official announcement: "The plenum of the Central Committee of the Communist Party of the Soviet Union has accepted the request of Comrade Nikita Sergeyevich Khrushchev in respect of the discharge of his duties as First Secretary of the Party for reasons of advanced age and declining health. The plenum of the Central Committee of the Communist Party of the Soviet Union has chosen Comrade Leonid Ilyich Brezhnev for the post of First Secretary."

On this day of October 14, 1964, the Competent Authority is just like everyone else in the country. That's all anyone can talk about.

"Advanced age", "declining health": it's clear what this means. There has been a coup, and Khrush, as he is nicknamed with some condescension mingled with a touch of affection, has been forced to abdicate. Everything must have gone smoothly: the deposed leader handed in his resignation "voluntarily". It is obvious that the Competent Authority approved this manoeuvre.

"That's good news for us," Colonel Volkov decides.

"That's bad news for me," Abram Tertz realises, with his pessimistic sixth sense.

This winter will be cold.

Like many people, he cannot help being fond of Khrush – this feeling has spread since the announcement headlining all the newspapers. For it is a well-known fact that in this wretched country it is always the worst leaders who take root. If Khrush was sent packing, that means he wasn't all that nasty or a crook. He was frank, sincere and naive, that Khrush! And therefore vulnerable.

Khrush, whose nickname sounds like a June bug, on this day of October 14, 1964, is already sorely missed.

Despite Pasternak, despite the hunt for clandestine books, despite the "pederasts", Khrush was the breath of life. Destalinization. Millions of *zeks* coming home. The end of cloying fear, stuck like tar on your back and following you everywhere you went, day and night.

Khrush is also the period when Abram Tertz did not get caught.

And when he met the love of his life.

A golden age!

"It's a shame our child won't be born under the good star of Khrush," he laments.

Only three more months to go. His wife's belly is perfectly round.

There's a little guy cooking in there who was conceived under Khrushchev – that's already a good start. He should count himself lucky. No-one will be able to say that he's completely Brezhnevian.

Brezhnev, when you see his lifeless face on all the front pages of the newspapers!

A placid mug that takes the wind out of everyone's sails. A quagmire.

"Well, I think he's quite good-looking, actually," Larissa says. "He's got such virile eyebrows."

Ivanov is annoyed at this unseemly comment. What do a man's eyebrows have to do with his political rectitude? He is emphatic:

"The Party is right. It's Brezhnev we need right now. The son of a metalworker."

The newspapers report on his feats of arms during the war – he was a political commissar.

One day, a ferry with the colonel on board hit a floating mine. Sailors dived into the water to save him.

Another day, as the Germans were approaching the Soviet positions, he saw the manoeuvre and ordered the soldiers to open fire with the heavy artillery, forcing the enemy to retreat.

He was wounded and decorated with the Order of the Red Flag.

Like all competent officers, Ivanov quickly learns the new boss' biography and forgets the old one's. What's the use of living in the past? Let us move forward into the new era! Let us put our trust in our new guardian angel!

He's right: love works best when it is reciprocated. As soon as the new master feels their devotion, funds are unblocked. The light bulbs now get changed more quickly. The worn-out carpet is replaced. The grumpy doormen too. Toilet bowls are at last installed in the operatives' lavatories. Volkov was right: they are being cosseted. Romance is blossoming between the Competent Authority and Brezhnev.

Ivanov now has an Erica all of his own. And the supplies to go with it. Hundreds of ink ribbons (even twin spool ones, black and red). Reams of carbon paper!

New filing cupboards, more sturdy, practical ones. With a hanging file system, just as in the West.

A new Xerox 914, bought by the Russian embassy in Vienna and dispatched via special container to Moscow, is enthroned in a specially fitted-out room.

Seven copies per minute. On ordinary paper! With diabolical precision.

The high-ranking officers queue up to have a turn playing with the marvel.

It breaks down a week after it is installed.

Everyone still comes and admires it anyway.

No surprise then that the morale of the troops is on the rise again. Forgotten are the misadventures of Novocherkassk, the exhausting routine of tracking down dealers, the endless surveillance of loonies swapping poems by Mandelstam.

You sleep better at night and see a more handsome face in the mirror.

You arrive at the office intent on changing the world.

And you take particular pleasure in paying attention to details.

Which is why Investigator Pakhmonov, on receiving *Redemption*, Nikolai Arzhak's latest book, from Washington, reads it with more care than usual.

It's a strange tale. There's something about it that feels like *déjà-vu*. The story of two friends, Felix and Victor. Felix is arrested and sent to prison – we're at the end of the 1940s. During his years in the labour camp, he cogitates (as did Kabo and Bregel) and comes to the erroneous conclusion that Victor is the only one who could have informed on him.

Coming back from the Gulag after the amnesty, Felix harasses Victor – just as Kabo came to haunt Monocle. Then he accuses him publicly, and tells his version of the events to anyone who cares to listen. (What an arsehole that Felix is! Pakhmonov thinks.) That's when the story takes a surprising turn. Although he is innocent, Victor does not protest. He feels that, like everyone else, he is "at fault for not obstructing anything". He does nothing to defend himself: everybody therefore assumes he is guilty. His fiancée leaves him. His professional life is ruined. He ends up in an asylum. Annihilated by a ricochet off collective guilt. (What a pansy! Pakhmonov thinks.)

The investigator closes the book and immediately talks to Ivanov about it, for Victor's misadventures seem to bear a direct relation to a recent case he had heard something about.

"Crikey!" Ivanov is startled.

Arzhak's novel is a retelling of what happened to Monocle.

Except that the colours of the story seem to be reversed, as in a photographic negative. Victor is innocent of what he is accused of, whereas Monocle is guilty. Victor's fiancée can't stand the idea of staying with a *seksot*, whereas Monocle's wife is perfectly content to do so. Victor is happy to be a scapegoat to expiate a collective sin, whereas Monocle is in denial of his own personal vice. But it is still obvious that, in its overarching plot as well as in the psychological details, it's the same story.

Impossible that it's a coincidence.

They check the publication date: it is earlier than the notorious public viva where Monocle was shot down in full flight. Given the time required to pass a manuscript to the West and the technical delays for publishing, we must deduce that… we must deduce…

Arzhak knew about Monocle's secret activity before everyone else, and about the role that he played in the Bregel and Kabo affair.

We need to look for Arzhak in Monocle's immediate circle.

We're on a serious trail.

Pakhmonov even wonders "What if he was actually Arzhak?"

That would take the cake.

Ivanov points out that this is impossible. The Competent Authority has been running Monocle under personal supervision for years. Countless cases have been opened thanks to his sound information. Our *seksot* takes so much pleasure in denouncing his comrades that you can't imagine anything would motivate him to self-sabotage like that.

Pakhmonov is not necessarily convinced, but, in the following days, a copy of the original manuscript arrives via the Soviet embassy in Washington – an agent of influence managed to get hold of it from the printers. A superior quality copy, made on a Xerox 914, where you can clearly identify the characteristics of the typewriter that was originally used. They compare it with Monocle's typewriter (there's no lack of reports). The scientific analysis establishes it: Monocle is not Arzhak.

Naturally they think of Kabo and Bregel.

"That's absurd," Pakhmonov says. "Knowing that his novel is already in the West, what interest would Bregel-Arzhak have in publicly ridiculing Monocle with that performance at the university, if it meant that he would be unmasked at the same time? No, no, no. Let me remind you that they already have ten years in the Gulag between them. That tends to cool hotheads down a bit."

They still follow that lead, with no results. Kabo and Bregel both have typewriters, but a swift investigation shows that they have nothing in common with the one used to commit the crime.

But that does not discourage the Competent Authority. Quite the contrary.

If it's not Kabo… If it's not Bregel…

"No rushing in as we did with Oksman," Brigade-General Zubov warns them, when he learns they're making progress.

Zubov is part of general command, so he ranks higher than Colonel Volkov – the Tertz–Arzhak affair is now well and truly classified as "A".

"Take it gently," he says. "And make sure you round up all of this mob for me in an iron maw."

Hercule Pakhmonov and Sherlock Ivanov take stock.

They summon Monocle, get him to replay the film of his ghosts again. Bregel. 1954. In the library, nothing happens,

Monocle flees. Then at the cafeteria, Monocle goes to say hello to him, and Bregel refuses to shake his hand.

"Who was present?"

"My friends, people from my group. Other students. The cafeteria is always packed."

Pakhmonov and Ivanov are insistent:

"Think, for Chrissake!"

Monocle remembers: the atmosphere was heavy. Awkward. Needing to justify himself in front of his friends whose eyes were questioning him. He'd had to take a light bantering tone, to try to fob them off: "I don't understand. Bregel thinks that I have something to do with his Gulag stuff. He's crazy, you know, he's completely insane!"

Either Arzhak was present at the time, or someone who was a direct witness told him about the scene.

They spend the next few days drawing from the well of Monocle's memory. Who was in his circle in 1954–5? In what circumstances? Monocle is floundering. Usually he has excellent skills at retaining the compromising things that his friends say, and delivering them to the right forwarding address, but now he can hardly even concentrate. As if the art that he practices on others doesn't work when he tries to apply it to himself. You know what they say about the shoemaker…

"I don't know, guys. I just can't remember."

To the shame of having perhaps frequented Arzhak without realising it – he of all people, the *seksot* among *seksots* – is added that of seeing the disappointment in his protectors' eyes.

"I've lost my touch," Monocle realises, and collapses.

Then he remembers that he had already thought about

the Arzhak problem. It was two years ago, after the broadcast on Radio Liberty. That thief had stolen his idea about the public murder day.

Pakhmonov can't believe his ears.

"You had the idea of one of Arzhak's books? You did?"

Monocle is almost offended.

Why shouldn't he be able to find good subjects? Like lots of other people, he too has a literary mind. An artistic sensibility.

"Except that you don't have the balls," Pakhmonov chuckles.

Everyone (except Monocle) is in an excellent mood. They can feel the fish getting closer to the net.

"But I mean, you should have reported that fact to us immediately," Ivanov says irritably.

"I thought it was a coincidence."

Better late than never. Come on, let's get back to work, make up for lost time.

Make lists, explore, eliminate.

The lists get shorter, the days get shorter too.

"I don't know, I still don't know," Monocle keeps repeating.

A superhero who has lost his superpowers would not be more of a cot case.

Suddenly Pakhmonov, who is a fine psychologist, as an investigator should be, has an epiphany.

"People avoid committing crimes when they know there's a rat around. It's instinctive. If I were Arzhak, I would try to keep my distance from Monocle before getting involved in any anti-Soviet activities."

They then focus on Monocle's old friends, those who

were in his close circle at the beginning of the 1950s, but with whom he's lost touch.

There's his childhood friend Andrei. The literature professor and Picasso expert, forever away with the fairies. They went to high school together. He now sports a rectangular beard, Russian style, and looks like an Orthodox priest.

Then there's Yuli, the translator. Charming and bohemian.

The connections slackened as time went by.

Monocle has scarcely seen Andrei since 1960. It's strange. They were very close, but now Andrei always has an excuse to refuse his invitations. "Too much work at uni, it's exam period." "I'm past my deadline for an article I'm writing." "Architecture in Asia is not my cup of tea." Yeah, right!

One of the last times he saw him was at Pasternak's funeral. Come to think of it, Yuli was there too.

Andrei Sinyavsky and Yuli Daniel.

Pakhmonov is pleased:

"Pasternak? Let's go and look at the photographs."

They surround themselves with the images gleaned by the operatives. They look for the man with the rectangular beard. Surprise! He's one of the tosspots carrying the lid of the coffin. And the other one is... Yuli Daniel.

"I want their complete biographies on my desk by this evening!" Pakhmonov says excitedly.

Elementary, really, when you have an efficient filing system, with multiple entry points.

In fact, Andrei Sinyavsky is not unknown to the Competent Authority. His father, Donat, was arrested in '51, accused of being a Western spy for distributing American aid to famine victims in '22. He was released (by some miracle) six months later.

You can see how that might have led to his anti-Soviet views, our fine sleuths observe.

Another detail is capital: in the archives they find the name of Hélène Peltier, that French daughter of a military attaché. In 1947, the budding relationship between Hélène and Andrei was duly noted and documented, and we even thought it might come in handy one day: spying on the admiral indirectly through his daughter's admirers. The young lady having lost interest in her Russian beau (did she sense the danger?), the plan flopped. She returned to the Soviet Union only after 1954.

"I want to know all of Hélène Peltier's movements in our country since that date."

Nothing could be simpler, when every single tourist is supervised. In theory at least. For there has been some regrettable laxity in this practice since the country partly opened itself up to foreigners, in the euphoria of the "thaw".

"We were understaffed!" Ivanov pleads, when shown the blind spots and gaps in the monitoring of Hélène Peltier.

Our reports show that she came to Moscow several times and that she manoeuvred in the circle of the university literature department.

The pathways taken by the manuscripts become clear. Sinyavsky is the key player. Whether he is Arzhak or Tertz doesn't matter, the man supplied the contraband to Peltier, who then passed it to an accomplice at the French embassy – we have the confirmation that she went there frequently.

Then the anti-Soviet prose left the territory in the diplomatic pouch.

"Let's put Sinyavsky and Daniel under operational constraint."

"Operational constraint" means there's work to be done. You have to understand all their networks. Carry out a field investigation. Listen to their telephone conversations. Read their post. Place microphones in their apartments. And you have to tail them, of course.

The ideal would be to neutralise them at the very moment they are handing over a manuscript to that Hélène Peltier woman.

Otherwise, we have to collect all the facts, the coincidences.

We could take the risk of searching their apartments in their absence, as we did with Penkovsky.

Pros: if you discover a compromising manuscript, the deal is in the bag, you can arrest them without further ado.

Cons: intellectuals' apartments are stuffed with papers. Try figuring out what needs to be read in a shithouse like that! While our operatives are good at finding caches of foreign currency or spying equipment, they are lost when faced with mountains of writing to analyse. It's impossible to do it quickly, and especially to put everything back where you found it.

"Let's hurry up and take our time," the investigator decrees. "Even if we just have to wait for the Peltier woman to go and climb into the bear's mouth. Now that we have them in our sights, they won't fly away, those two birdies."

XIX

In November 1964, the operational constraint is in place.

We rapidly get the names of the friends from the inner circle. There's the art historian Igor Golomstock, the linguist Andrei Menshutin and his wife Lydia, the poet Andrei Sergeev and his wife Lyudochka, the high school teacher Emma Shitova, the icon restorer Kolya Kishilov. Then there's Viktor Duvakin, the incredible Mayakovsky specialist: give him any random date in the calendar and he can tell you what the poet was doing on that day.

There's also young Volodya Vysotsky, who often comes to the house with his guitar to sing gangland songs.

Masha, Sinyavsky's wife, records him on a reel-to-reel tape recorder.

The Competent Authority records the Sinyavskys recording Vysotsky.

This bard, this Vysotsky, already has a proper file, of course. He has just graduated from the Moscow Arts Theatre school, and already been involved in countless piss-ups and scandals.

When Vysotsky starts bellowing out his songs, the walls shake. The microphone concealed in the ceiling lamp is saturated. His husky voice is like a storm on the Baltic Sea:

I have my guitar – walls, step aside!
I'll see no freedom all life long, because of evil fortune!
Slit my throat, slit my veins,
Just don't break my silver strings!

The Competent Authority wonders what should be done about it. The lyrics aren't anti-Soviet if you read them literally, and God knows our experts have read and re-read them over and over again, but the attitude! Why does he have to bawl like a drunkard? What's the point of singing about prison all the time, of pretending he's a jailbird?

You have to admit that the man also bellows out songs about the Great Patriotic War, and they do grab you by the guts, as Nikonovich reflects.

"Guts, skeletons or optic nerves, I don't care, just erase your recordings quick smart," Pakhmonov orders.

Vysotsky spreading around the staff is all we need!

"Tell me instead what the suspect is actually talking about. Have you learnt anything more?"

Nothing to speak of, in a month's listening.

Topic of conversation number one is the baby, who is expected at the end of December. The Sinyavskys are convinced it will be a boy. They want to give him a simple name, something very Russian, very rural.

"What a good idea," Kulakov approves.

"They should call him Ivan," Pakhmonov says. "You can't get more traditional than that."

"That's a bit dopey, though, isn't it? Ivan, Ivanushka?" Kulakov wonders.

Lieutenant Ivanov, who has always had a slight inferiority

complex because of the banality of his last name, cringes a bit.

Out of superstition, Sinyavsky cuts any conversations about names short:

"Let's wait until he's born, then we'll see."

"He's right!" Ivanov says, in spite of himself.

For a while now, he and Larissa have been doing the same thing, by tacit agreement. Because, the more you want something, the more ideas you give to bad luck, which, it's a well-known fact, does everything in its power to hit you where it hurts. Sometimes Ivanov thinks they should never have blabbed so carelessly about how much they wanted a child.

When they're not talking about baby clothes, the Sinyavskys discuss Pasternak. And that's where our discreet ears prick up. Except that you can't understand a thing the suspects are saying. Poetry, poetry, poetry. It's enough to make Kulakov dizzy. But it becomes clear that Sinyavsky is writing something about Pasternak.

"We've got him!"

The euphoria is short-lived, however. The intelligence gathered shows that there is nothing political about this. An anthology of Pasternak's poetry is being prepared by the very serious Soviet Writer publishing house, in the prestigious "Library of the Poets" series. In the most official way possible, Andrei Sinyavsky, as the pre-eminent specialist of Pasternak, was invited to write a long introduction.

"I don't understand a thing anymore," Kulakov complains. "One day Pasternak is O.K., the next it's the opposite. Make up your mind."

He's not wrong there.

"It's not our job to assess the quality of Pasternak's poetry," Pakhmonov reassures him. "Everyone has their own cross to bear. We are here to see that the instructions are applied."

"Fuck, it does your head in, Pasternak does."

Everyone agrees.

Including Sinyavsky, who is wondering how to navigate between the shoals of censorship so that he can somehow put together an introduction that doesn't misrepresent the great poet's work. If he doesn't manage that, the publication of the book can be cancelled, quite simply. Which must not be allowed to happen: this will be the first full-length anthology of Pasternak's work to be published in the Soviet Union, and thus, *de facto*, a rehabilitation of the poet after his death and only five years after his works were banned.

Sinyavsky fights for every sentence, to the last word. There's an incessant exchange of mail with the heads of the publishing house, where, despite the senior editors' good will, everyone fears for their necks. Why does Sinyavsky not clearly say that "Pasternak was incapable of becoming an active fighter for socialism", as he is being begged to do? Is it so hard for him to comply with the traditional editorial line that never dissociates art from politics? Why doesn't he mention *Doctor Zhivago* (and how Pasternak was criticised for it, as he should be) when the affair is of public notoriety? "I must inform you, with all possible sincerity, clarity, and responsibility, that the book's publication depends only on your goodwill in including the requested changes to your introduction," writes Vladimir Orlov, the project leader.

The Pasternakian choice is therefore as follows: either

Sinyavsky revises his introduction and criticises Pasternak's "political" positions, or the book, which is of capital importance to Russian culture, will never see the light of day.

Engaging in symbiosis through their ears, the Competent Authority starts to discuss literature.

Ivanov is indignant:

"I can't see why he's not doing what is being asked of him. It's a proof of his latent anti-Soviet attitude."

"Maybe he wants to sabotage the publication of Pasternak, which wouldn't be a bad outcome actually," Kulakov muses.

The good thing about Kulakov is that he's not afraid of being taken for an idiot.

Pakhmonov, the most literary-minded of them all, has a less naive view of things:

"He's a crafty fox."

Sinyavsky has understood that you can't just ignore Pasternak, otherwise we look like a horrible totalitarian regime. The intelligentsia all over the world can't stop nagging us: Pasternak, Pasternak, Pasternak. And so we give the authorisation to publish a book of innocent poems. So that you can say: "Pasternak? What about Pasternak? Here you go, there's your idol for you!" And Sinyavsky is making the most of this to push the limits.

"He's taking advantage of our weakness, he is," Shmakov groans.

"Not exactly. He has understood that we need a small dose of Pasternak, and he's being pernickety. You'll see, they'll give in to all of his demands in the end."

That a citizen could find himself in a position of power (well, relative power) in relation to the representatives (even distant representatives) of the State makes Shmakov choke, he who is nothing but obedient:

"That arsehole threatened to abandon the whole project!"

Pakhmonov shrugs.

"He's cunning, that Sinyavsky! That's why it's interesting to observe him under operational constraint. I wonder how he will behave during his first interrogation, once we've got him… *Tsap*! *Tsap-tsarap*!

And he mimes a cat's paw putting out its claws.

On the other side of the microphone, Sinyavsky shivers:

"I saw two black cats today. The first one tried to cross the road in front of me, but then changed its mind. The other one looked at me with its yellow eyes, from up on a wall. No good, no good at all. I think they'll get me, Masha."

"We've known from the very beginning they'll get you. We're prepared."

Sinyavsky obviously needs comfort: you can hear a bottle clinking on the lip of a glass. He's drinking. He's drinking a lot.

Pakhmonov and the others play the recording over and over again.

Kulakov is triumphant:

"'I think they'll get me' – that's us he's talking about. If he's afraid of being arrested, that means he's guilty."

Pakhmonov is unperturbed:

"Calm down. He could just as soon be talking about the editors of the Poets' Library or his knucklehead students. That's not evidence."

Another day, they record the following statement:

"Abram Tertz is one hell of a tightrope walker," Sinyavsky says, shuffling papers as if he were reading something.

And he sings the gangsters' song to go along with it:
Abrashka Tertz, the pickpocket of legend,
And Sonya-the-whore, who shines throughout the land…

"He's pissed," is Ivanov's instant diagnosis.

"And it's not really a confession anyway," is Pakhmonov's appraisal. "Half of Moscow, especially in literary circles, knows about Abram Tertz by now. Oksman used to read him too."

Then the microphone, for some unknown reason, stops working.

"He's onto us!" Kulakov frets.

Impossible to replace it now: Masha is eight months pregnant, and hardly leaves the house anymore.

When they finally manage to do so, they find that the equipment is burnt out. Vapour had condensed along the wire and got into the heart of the device. Sinyavsky, after boiling himself an egg on a little portable gas burner, had forgotten to turn the water off.

When the listening starts up again, there's nothing but materialist preoccupations and prenatal anxiety crushing all conversation.

"My wife was freaking out like that too, before our first one," Pakhmonov says, the happy sire of three children.

Thus fly the days of December, and freeze the legs of the operatives staked out in the cars beneath the windows.

She's in labour, at last!

The operatives were bored stiff with waiting, now they are as frisky as young puppies in the first winter snow: they discreetly photograph everyone bringing little messages of congratulation to the young mother while she is stuck in the maternity hospital.

"They called him Iegor!" Kulakov booms.
And suddenly everyone turns into gossipy old wives.
"That's a nice Slavic name."
"It's a dope's name, that's what it is."
"Well, you can't get more Russian than that, now, can you?"
"'Here comes Iegor, three inches off the floor.'"
"'Grandad Iegor, do keep your cock indoors.'"
"It's somehow even more Russian than Ivan."
"No way!"
"Yes, it is. It comes from George, the patron saint of Russia."
"And how do you know that, then?"
"I've got two priests in my network. You'd never believe the stuff I learn. In fact Yuri also comes from George. Iegor, Yuri, George, same thing."

As the days go by, every single event in this new little Muscovite's life is duly commented on:

"They don't have a crib: Iegor is sleeping in a suitcase."

"They got an Orthodox priest to come by for a home baptism."

"It's a catastrophe: the doctors are saying the baby boy is blind. He's not reacting to light. The Sinyavskys are distraught."

"False alarm! It's just that he's lost in thought, the little ratbag. A hyper-competent paediatrician made a house call: he says that Iegor sees perfectly."

"Emile Liuboshitz. Take a note of that name, just in case anyone ever needs a paediatrician."

"Vysotsky dropped by. He gave them his own son's cradle, coz he's grown out of it now. They took the opportunity to make some more recordings. Still criminals' songs."

"Iegor is in the emergency room with a temperature of 40°C. He's got bad diarrhoea."

"He's so frail!"

"He's not being breastfed anymore!"

———

At last the winter warms up slightly. The little family's outings become more frequent. They go to the same houses, to visit the same friends. The Competent Authority knows them all by heart now. You've never seen a chump so easy to tail. Sinyavsky never hurries – and with his great big beard, it's impossible to lose sight of him. He doesn't suspect a thing, he always lets people pass in front of him, you can have fun doing "eyes in the back of the head" as much as you like with him, it's a piece of cake.

His wife, Maria Vasilyevna Rozanova, is just the opposite. Lively, unpredictable, always a sarcastic smile on her lips, you sometimes get the disagreeable sense that she's the one following you. She's capable of suddenly dashing across eight lanes of traffic on Gorky Avenue without looking at the cars. It's just as well she's now laden with Iegor, who slows her down considerably.

Today all three of them are having lunch with an old friend from university.

The caretaker of the building, a fine fellow seriously wounded in the war, rings the doorbell: he has a package to deliver.

They ask him in, when he says:

"What about your mates outside, aren't you inviting them up?"

"What mates? Who are you talking about?"

Something like a wave of sadness washes over the caretaker's face when he understands.

"Come to the window, let me show you. Careful. Don't touch the curtain. Have a look, over there, under the lean-to. Two guys smoking. You don't know them? Well then, I regret to inform you that you are being shadowed. I was a liaison agent myself in the border guards, during the war. I know their techniques. I mean, I'm telling you this, I'm telling you nothing. Have a good day anyway!"

It's like the world has come crumbling down.

Sinyavsky, his legs like lead, can't move off the couch.

We've been found out. They know. That's the end of our carefree life.

Rozanova, playfully:

"Let's do an amusing experiment to confirm this hypothesis. I'll go out to make a call from the phone booth, and you can observe how the two clowns behave from up here."

She might as well be clapping, she's so excited.

At last some action, after years of waiting!

She goes out of the building, passes in front of the lean-to, turns into the street. One of the guys immediately stubs out his cigarette and follows in her tracks. The other one stays where he is, in observation.

When she comes back ten minutes later, so does the trailing shadow. The test is positive.

"We need to hold a war council and adjust our behaviour," Rozanova says. "They might have found you out, but they haven't arrested you yet. Or even summoned you for an interview. That means they're still looking. We need to get word to Hélène immediately that she isn't to set foot in the Soviet Union again."

At home, they now make an effort to talk only about ordinary things. Sometimes they stop dead in the middle of a sentence, and raise an index finger to the invisible ears hiding in the ceiling: careful, we're being listened to!

They have a dog, a black spaniel. An excellent pretext to go outside in the evenings. In the street, no-one can hear or record them.

"I just hope I don't turn out like my father," Sinyavsky blurts out. "When he was released and put under house arrest in a village in the provinces, he went round the bend. He was convinced the intelligence agencies could read his mind, from a distance, as soon as he went anywhere near a power pole. He didn't ever talk at home anymore. It was only when he was a few miles into the forest that he would unclench his teeth."

Over the course of their walks, they develop a strategy.

Clear out the apartment as best they can, liquidating all compromising traces. Destroy all the old manuscripts and notes.

"Well that's easily done, I haven't written anything for over a year." Sinyavsky sighs. "Except a few impromptu thoughts."

"There's no way we're throwing everything out because of those bastards," Rozanova says. "Let's hide everything with Tutankhamen."

That's what they call the hiding place behind the bookcase, Tutankhamen's secret chamber, where they pile up all the copies of *Esprit*, the various editions of Abram Tertz, the correspondence with Pasternak.

Rozanova pulls the string for the lightbulb, closes up the tomb. She rubs the metal hinges with brown shoe polish. Nothing shines anymore, nothing stands out. Then she seals it off for good with a nail.

Sinyavsky is dumbfounded by his wife's madcap energy. How does she do it? For him, it's impossible to go on living serenely while dangling over the abyss. Writing is even more impossible.

Georgian cognac, on the other hand... Vodka... It's like a natural temptation. Unlike some people who become more gregarious with drink, Sinyavsky becomes even more introverted. He finds his way to the couch and falls asleep like an innocent halfwit. Flat on his stomach, his nose stuck into his beard, snoring away.

"What's wrong with him?" Ivanov worries. "He's not even forty yet. A successful professional career, a great reputation, well known in university and critical circles. Destroying himself like that. What moral weakness! What self-indulgence!"

Kulakov has an explanation.

"It's hard to live with a feeling of guilt. Especially when you have betrayed the Union of Soviet Socialist Republics."

Rozanova loses her temper too:

"You have no right to do this! Get a grip, you wimp!" And, lowering her voice so as not to be heard by the big ears: "Abram Tertz is supposed to be forged of another kind of metal. He laughs in the face of danger!"

"Leave me alone, I'm not Abram Tertz," he whispers calmly. "I'm not even up to his knees."

And he collapses and snores some more.

Another time (we're in May 1965 now), at the birthday party of a distant acquaintance, he goes haywire. After being taciturn during the whole meal, and mixing cognac with champagne in his glass, all of a sudden Andrei Sinyavsky stands up and raises a toast to Abram Tertz. Adding, with a dark smile:

"For Abram Tertz is me!"

The entire party petrifies. Nobody laughs, thinking it's a joke. It's as if there's a dumbbell inside each piece of cake. Nobody even remembers to light the candles.

The stunt is stupid: he doesn't even know half the people there. And it's a universal law of Soviet society that in a company of twenty people you don't know, there's always one nark.

By dumb luck, not this time. Perhaps also because it was so unpleasant to watch that pisshead ridicule himself in public by claiming to be who he clearly wasn't – for the real Abram Tertz would never be stupid enough to declare it openly. Was there something of the exhausted animal there, at the end of the chase, lying down to let itself die, so much so that even the hunter loses the urge to stand up and finish it off?

The veterinarians of the Competent Authority would have had no such scruples. Ah, if only they had known!

At the end of May, the famous anthology of Pasternak's poems finally comes out. Don't be fooled by its gloomy washed-out blue cover – it's a firecracker. Stocks in the Moscow bookshops are swept away by a tidal wave of buyers. The print run of only 40,000 copies means Sinyavsky has all the trouble in the world getting his own author's copies. He consoles himself by queueing for smoked sprats, of which he manages to snap up five tins.

That way he won't be drinking on an empty stomach.

The file of the investigation is getting thicker. Its branches are covered with lush green leaves, the fruits promise to be delicious.

The painstaking enquiry and thorough cross-checking on Hélène Peltier confirm what Pakhmonov already knew. Even better, sources close to Gallimard start blabbing: in the autumn of 1956, not content with assisting Abram Tertz in committing his crime, she also served as the mule for a manuscript of *Doctor Zhivago* destined for publication in France. Apparently she worked on the translation too. No name appears on the title page of the French edition, precisely to keep the identity of the intermediaries secret. Revealing them would have led inescapably to the compromising of all their Russian correspondents, including Abram Tertz.

"What a silly little bourgeois girl!" Pakhmonov rages, on seeing a photograph of Hélène, smiling in her string of fat pearls. "But what a pain in the arse!"

We consider the idea of bringing her to the Soviet Union, to then *tsap*! *tsarap*! We set up a phoney cultural event, all expenses paid, with Pasternak's poetry and promises of "literary discussions" on the menu, but curiously Hélène Peltier ignores the morsel of cheese. She doesn't even deign to answer a follow-up by a colleague at the University of Toulouse.

"We won't catch her," Pakhmonov concludes. "She is on her guard."

That's rather strange.

The Competent Authority also can't help noticing that no new information about Sinyavsky has been discovered for a while now. He always sees the same people – Golomstock, Menshutin, Kishilov… Daniel a bit less – as if they were avoiding each other. His private conversations at home are of dazzling banality. He frequently walks his spaniel with his wife, sometimes up to five times a day.

Pakhmonov jumps.

"Five times a day? Are you sure?"

"Affirmative, Sir."

"Five times is far too much for a dog. They've caught on that they're being listened to!"

It is long since time to act.

XX

Seasoned operatives all know this: the best day to pick up an important suspect is Wednesday. Fridays and Thursdays are to be avoided – too close to the weekend. What with offices closing, leave requests approved, and a vagabond spirit in the air, whether you like it or not, the rhythm of the interrogation slackens. There's not the same pressure. That gives the suspect the opportunity to catch his breath, just when the shock of his arrest has made him vulnerable. A fellow can get stubborn, and then the custody period can drag on, wasting everyone's time.

With this focus on maximum pressure, Mondays and Tuesdays are not bad days either of course, but it just so happens that the beginning of the week is the perfect time to put the final touches on your paperwork and complete the planning of the operation. Get the most difficult tasks done on the first day of the week, says the philosopher. Dream about the success of the intervention in all its minute detail on Tuesday, act on Wednesday, work on Thursday, Friday and Saturday. Savour your results on Sunday. Ideally situated, Wednesday is the critical point when you can take action.

It's perfect timing in fact. On Wednesday mornings,

Sinyavsky gives a literary studies lecture to future actors at the Moscow Arts Theatre school – that's where he made friends with young Vysotsky. He leaves his apartment around 9 a.m. He's alone in the street, without his wife or kid hanging around. It's ideal. No embarrassing scenes, no boo-hoos. You can contain the emotional trauma – and not just for the suspect either. Operatives sometimes also become less clear-headed in these delicate situations. That's why, contrary to what a novice might think, an arrest at the suspect's residence is not actually the most practical option. We're not under (you know who) anymore, when we would show up late in the evening or in the middle of the night, banging on the doors with our big boots, making the whole building shudder. In the street, in broad daylight, the arrest is efficient – and modern too.

Sinyavsky is heading for the trolleybus station. He's late, walking fast. Our provident cream-coloured car is already parked on Nikitskie Vorota Square. Here he comes now, with his cigarette. Two undercover operatives are standing among the passengers, pretending to wait for the trolleybus too. Sinyavsky looks at his watch. He doesn't suspect a thing.

"Andrei Donatovich Sinyavsky?"

The best way to proceed is to approach the suspect from behind and to call him by his name. It is advisable to add a little friendly warmth to your voice, as if you were meeting an old acquaintance or university professor by chance.

He turns around, surprised. He is slightly off balance. As if by magic, the cream-coloured car has materialised a few inches away from him. And so all our operatives have to do is gently push him towards the wide open door.

"Come with us, Andrei Donatovich. Important business."

Firmly and politely. From inside the car, helpful hands grab his briefcase, as if to help him get in. In the blink of an eye, he is sitting on the back seat. Two operatives are jammed in next to him, one on either side. The door slams, we've caught the birdie. The car starts up – easy now, no rush. This is not the movies. Here, time obeys us.

Without brutality but with the determination of a concrete slab, the operatives hold down the suspect's arms on his lap. Just so he knows who's boss. Not that it would occur to him to try and escape, no. One of them pulls the fag out of his mouth, flicks it out the window.

"Smoking is forbidden in this car, Andrei Donatovich."

That's not entirely true – the ashtray is full of butts. Captain Nikonovich smokes like a factory. He's allowed. But not the suspect. You have to understand this nuance, which, in point of fact, is fairly elementary. The suspect has lost control of his entire existence, that's all there is to it. His life no longer belongs to him. From now on, we're the ones who decide where, how and at what time. That's why our instructions are to avoid talking. The car moves forward, not a word spoken. Operative Vasilyev searches Sinyavsky's briefcase, opens up the zippered pockets, looks through all the papers.

It must be action stations on all fronts inside the suspect's noggin. "What do they know?" Well, everything, old boy, everything! And what we don't know, you're about to tell us, now that your salad days of impunity are over.

"This is a mistake…" Sinyavsky attempts with a blank voice. "I appear to have been… arrested? You have no right, without a warrant. Do you have a warrant? Show me the warrant."

It's hilarious. All prisoners, down to the last man, make an attempt at bravado. It must be an involuntary reflex. While the ground is vanishing beneath their feet and, on a scale of one to ten, their scaredometer is at shitless, they still try to put up a good front. As if they know the law. As if they have nothing to hide. And they're not terrified. Who do they think they are kidding?

"Shut up!" Vasilyev barks. "You'll talk when we ask you to! You're not at the Moscow Arts Theatre school here!"

This remark causes general hilarity.

A few minutes later, it's a very quiet car that pulls up to the entrance of the Lubyanka.

So many people are here to greet him! From all the offices of all the directorates, inquisitive heads poke out: guys, we're bringing in Abram Tertz! Not even Rokotov caused such a commotion. And Penkovsky was hardly even noticed.

We got him in the end! Let's have a look at him, then! What's the writer like?

To be sure, he is anything but ordinary with his rectangular beard, his crossed eyes, his fingers yellowed by cigarettes.

"Get away now, this isn't the circus!" Pakhmonov orders, while feeling some satisfaction at the effect produced by his new "protégé". "Everyone back to your posts! Come in, Andrei Donatovich, if you please."

Only the intimate circle stays: Ivanov, Kulakov, Nikonovich.

"We find ourselves obliged to keep you with us for a short time, Andrei Donatovich. Do you understand? This doesn't come as a surprise to you, now does it? You know why you are here, don't you? Come now, don't be childish."

To begin with, as usual, you don't tell the suspect clearly what the reason for his "summons" is. You wait. You let him stew in his conscience. In his fear.

"What do you think the reasons might be for us to arrest a respectable citizen, a remarkable professor, a notable literary critic, just like that, in the middle of the street? Tell us, Andrei Donatovich. Explain this to me. Because I don't understand."

This first phase is rather amusing. And in fact Pakhmonov is in a very good mood. He's enjoying hamming up the role of the omniscient type.

An hour goes by. Still beating around the bush.

"It's best that you come clean, Andrei Donatovich. I'll let you in on a secret. When the suspect admits spontaneously, that creates attenuating circumstances that can go as far as cancelling the initial penalty. I shouldn't be telling you this, in fact, but you seem like a nice guy. Really. I even attended one of your lectures. It was about Mayakovsky, our great, our magnificent poet. I was at the back of the room, you didn't notice me. I like to read, you see. Tolstoy, Chekhov…"

Find a connection so you can pretend to be empathetic.

Sinyavsky then allows himself his first inner smile: he always thought Tolstoy was a deadbeat, too stuck-up and moralistic. And as for Chekhov, well, he can talk about him for hours. Now's his opportunity!

"The dynamic of the plot, in Chekhov, often rests on an artifice of some kind, such as the imminence of a character's departure on a journey. In fact in "The Lady with the Dog", if you remember…"

That story is a classic that is always on the school curriculum, so you can be sure that Pakhmonov has read it.

But contrary to what Pakhmonov might have led the suspect to believe, Chekhov is not his abiding passion. And we are not in a lecture hall at the Institute here. Sinyavsky does not seem to notice that his learned monologue falls flat.

An hour passes.

And another hour.

Ivanov, Kulakov and Nikonovich go off to do the house search. It's time to get moving.

Faced with Sinyavsky's silence, the investigator pretends to beg him:

"Stop being so secretive and take a weight off your conscience, now. Be a good sport. We don't have all night."

The aim is to make the suspect think that you don't know that much about his innards after all.

A minuscule ray of hope then glimmers at the end of the corridor where all the doors are shut.

Which you finally sweep away with a resounding:

"Abram Tertz!"

Hurled into his face like a canon shot after three hours of running in place.

It is then quite pleasing to watch the forlorn hope in the suspect's eyes shatter.

But with Sinyavsky you've got to find those eyes first, he's so cross-eyed they're all over the place!

Still, you do get the sense of a wounded animal.

"We know everything, Sinyavsky. It's not even worth trying to pretend anymore. You'll just make a fool of yourself."

We know about Abram Tertz. Nikolai Arzhak too. Hélène Peltier, that was clever, but we got there in the end.

We have statements. Irrefutable proof! From places you don't even suspect exist!

That idea, a throwaway line at the end of the interrogation, stays with the suspect when he goes off to languish in his cell. He starts to brood: who supplied the information? Under what circumstances? Was it someone in France who couldn't hold their tongue? Did Hélène say too much without realising it? He's not surprised: the French can't help strutting around like peacocks. The more he goes round in circles, the more psychologically vulnerable he becomes.

Since he hasn't been told anything clearly, he doesn't yet know where the decisive blow will come from. He's having trouble building a defence strategy. He feels as if his handholds have been soaped, and when he thinks of Masha and Iegor, who must be wondering what tomorrow will bring, he is a hair's breadth away from panic.

Sinyavsky is not alone in his cell, of course. We've put a common crim in there with him – a non-violent one obviously, on the express request of Pakhmonov, because this suspect is far too precious. The common crim, with his simple manners, frank language, and propensity to conspire, is charged with making him talk, and reporting on it later.

It's not so much the material aspects of the crime that worry Pakhmonov, no, we have everything we need to prove that Sinyavsky is Abram Tertz. For Arzhak, it's even clearer: in the search of Yuli Daniel's apartment, we found the Optima typewriter that was used to type the manuscript of *Redemption*.

The significance of the crime, however, is subject to

interpretation. Article 70 sanctions the creation, preservation and distribution of "anti-Soviet productions", but here, only the creation is obvious. Preservation is difficult to prove: nothing really compromising has been found in the search. As for distribution, it is strictly limited to the West, unless we try to incriminate him for the readings he gave to his wife and closest friends.

And that's not the only worry.

The weakness of the charge lies in the anti-Soviet character of what was published.

How indeed do you prove that a fictional text defames the Soviet Union? Especially if the plot turns out to be fantasy. In what way can the capacity to guess the future, featured by the narrator of "Icy Weather", be said to contradict proletarian doctrine?

When you're a real communist, like Pakhmonov, Ivanov or Kulakov, you just know, you can feel it in your bones, it gives you the shivers, but *proving* it is another story altogether.

Unless the suspect himself confesses to his dark intentions.

If he tells his cellmate that yes, he hates the Soviet Union and its leaders, that yes, he abhors the ideology that goes with it, that yes, he wrote what he did to mock everything we hold sacred – there you go, he's cooked!

Sinyavsky persists in denying the evidence.

"*On Socialist Realism* is an aesthetic study, there's nothing political about it," he repeats at every interrogation.

Pakhmonov gets seriously annoyed:

"That's enough playing the fool! In *The Makepeace Experiment*, you have that repulsive passage where Lenin is ill and leaves his residence at night, and then you write 'if there was no-one about, he threw back his bald head and started to bay at the moon'!* You dare to write that about an ailing man, in the last few days of his life, which was entirely devoted to the happiness of the oppressed classes, and let me remind you it's not just anybody you're writing about, but the great Lenin! Do you realise?"

"In the novel, it's not me who's telling the story, but a soldier from his personal guard, a Chekist, who thought he saw Lenin at night. He was perhaps a victim of a hallucination, the story doesn't say."

Pakhmonov is outraged:

"What do you mean, it's not you…? I can read 'Abram Tertz' here on the cover. Admit it, Andrei Donatovich, instead of stupidly denying it. Have the courage of your own opinions."

"It's got nothing to do with courage," Sinyavsky tries for the umpteenth time. "The character who is speaking is not necessarily the author. It's a very common literary device. Take Chekhov, for example, in 'A Chameleon', you'll remember the policeman speaking is not Chekhov either…"

"Stop using Chekhov to support your fallacious arguments!"

You can't get anything out of him, that Sinyavsky.

To cap it all, his cellmate has now asked to borrow an anthology of Mayakovsky's poems. With Sinyavsky reciting them non-stop, he's caught the rhythm virus. *A Cloud in Trousers* has opened up unsuspected perspectives in his criminal mind. What is this miracle?

* *The Makepeace Experiment*, transl. Manya Harari (Harvill Press, first published 1965), p. 95

XXI

With the arrest of Abram Tertz and Nikolai Arzhak, the autumn of 1965 changes the colours of the world.

For a time, there are more sprats in the shops.

Other displays are empty. The anthology of Pasternak's poetry, with Sinyavsky's preface, is taken off the shelves of the very few bookshops which still had copies. The stocks are destroyed. A black market springs up at once, on Maurice Thorez Embankment. "Do you have Pasternak?" becomes the dealers' obsessive catch cry. A rumour goes round that a bookbinder at State Printing Press 5, in Leningrad, pilfered a few copies destined for the shredder and lived like a tsar for two years, until he was arrested for receiving "income unconnected with work".

Sinyavsky gets expelled from the Soviet Writers' Union, banished from the university, extracted from all literary journals. And yet, he has never been more present. He's the only person anyone talks about in Moscow's intellectual circles, in whispers between two doors.

"To think we all thought that Abram Tertz was a hoax!"

"Two writers arrested, for goodness' sake! We haven't seen anything like it since the Ogre."

"Who'll be next? Who?"

"We need to mobilise ourselves if we don't want to go back to the ice age."

"Are you crazy?"

A few hotheads take up their pens, write to *Izvestia* or the Supreme Soviet, demanding the release of Sinyavsky and Daniel. You systematically summon them for a good going-over, then you clip their wings by shooing them out with a broom from their jobs, studies, accommodation, Komsomol.

Seeing the protestors' files multiply, Ivanov thinks the country really is going to the dogs. People feel strong enough to provoke the State – it's as if Pandora's Box is no longer airtight.

"I told you so, Larissa!" Ivanov keeps saying. "Do you remember the Sokolniki exhibition? Utter madness!"

We let the opium of the West reach our lungs. Jazz, jeans and Picasso have undermined the moral principles of the weakest citizens. No wonder they're defending Abram Tertz now.

"It's mostly that you didn't have your priorities right," Larissa says. "Forgive me for meddling in what is not my business, especially since it's classified Secret, but if you had put all your resources on Hélène Peltier and her consorts, rather than hunting down imported contraband boxes of Bic Cristal pens, you would have lanced the boil in 1959."

"While letting the Soviet Union turn into a vast Sokolniki," Ivanov protests.

No, you need both. Ideological warfare is won by setting our sights on modesty in clothing, abstinence from gadgets, and, at the same time, thrashing protestors and literary Vlasovs. That's what we need to do from now on: advance on both legs.

While we wait for things to stabilise, there are the autumn storms to manage: a demonstration, yes, a demonstration in support of Sinyavsky and Daniel is planned for December 5, 1965, at 6 p.m., on Pushkin Square, in Moscow.

The Competent Authority is pinching itself: no, we're not dreaming. Organised by Soviet citizens themselves, with no instruction from the Party, a spontaneous demonstration, so to speak, propagated by word of mouth and a tract printed on a typewriter, it's unheard of since… the dawn of the twilight. Let's ask the old-timers – no, not one of them has ever seen anything so incredible.

So, a demonstration. Of about fifty people in total. Mostly students. Monitored by two hundred undercover operatives, including Ivanov. You let the kids unfurl their banner "Demand glasnost for the Sinyavsky-Daniel trial". The offense of anti-Soviet propaganda duly registered, you book them all good and proper.

"'Glasnost' – what do they mean by that?" Kulakov says, still in shock at this unimaginable impudence.

"Look it up in the dictionary," Ivanov snaps. "And don't forget to compile complete files on them, so they get what's coming to them. I want exemplary expulsions for the students. No community service!"

Ivanov is irritable because the work is piling up: he's losing track of all the articles in the foreign press. *Le Monde*, *The Lancet*, the *Washington Post*. Indignant reactions of intellectuals from all over the world. Getting more and more virulent.

And it's not just the press. Our diplomats are being confronted and our scientists and artists harassed, as soon as they cross the border. There are the hysterical types:

"Release Tertz!" The literary history buffs: "Even Pasternak was never arrested!" The legal experts: "The Soviet Criminal Code forbids neither publication abroad nor the use of a pseudonym!" You'd think all the capitalist riff-raff have rushed in to defend the traitors.

Even the P.E.N. Club of the Philippines has graced us with a telegram, addressed to the Soviet Writers' Union: "We are very disappointed by the arrest of the writers Sinyavsky and Daniel. We belong to the same fraternal group. We demand that you take all necessary measures with the authorised instances." How touching!

How are you supposed to sift through this avalanche? Or write reports? You'd need interns, offices, desks!

Cornered, Ivanov sends a request along those lines to higher management.

Forty-eight hours later, he's summoned by Colonel Volkov.

Congratulations: his call has been heard. Additional resources will be parachuted onto the affair. That comes from high up, very high up. A massive recruitment drive is planned. And to coordinate this busy beehive, he, Ivanov, is now promoted to department head for the analysis of foreign media.

Volkov confirms it: there is lots of constructive work to look forward to. We'll be able to respond blow by blow now. Let them protest if they feel like it! We'll make the most of it to draw up files on all the miscreants, which will allow us to keep them at a safe distance from society.

"I also am a great believer in re-education," Ivanov insists.

Colonel Volkov shrugs: "You sort it out."

That evening Ivanov and Larissa are reading Sholokhov's *Virgin Soil Upturned*. Two volumes of three hundred pages each. Kolkhozes as far as the eye can see.

"Are you sure this is really necessary?" Ivanov attempts.

The tender silence of his wife, who is already halfway through the second volume, convinces him in the end.

"You're right." He sighs. "It is essential reading."

"A dungy steam billowed out of the stable doors…"

If they are in such a hurry to finish the book, it's because they've just found out: the Academy in Stockholm has awarded Sholokhov the Nobel Prize for Literature.

In itself, the prize doesn't mean much – Pasternak got it too, after all. The political dimension of the Nobel is obvious, though, as any number of friends of the Soviet Union have emphasised: Jean-Paul Sartre, Louis Aragon. But with Sholokhov, it's different. This is excellent news. We'll be able to fight fire with fire.

There's nobody more loyal, more Soviet, than Sholokhov.

"He splashed in the frozen puddles as he walked, and stumbled over the icy clods of cow dung in the market square…"

You can smell the peasants in this book. The great school of socialist realism.

It was intellectual snobbery that made Sinyavsky write that pamphlet, Ivanov thinks. That town mouse, in his apartment stuffed with books, has never really worked with his hands. He's in for a shock when he gets to the penal colony.

"Davydov sat down at the table, told them of the tasks which the party had set in connection with the two-months' advance towards complete collectivisation, and proposed that a meeting of the poor Cossacks and active workers be called for the very next day…"*

While Sinyavsky and Daniel are being simmered at the Lubyanka, Sholokhov is in Stockholm.

He barely has time to drink a glass of champagne before someone shoves an official letter in his hands, from France. Signed by Maurice Blanchot, André Breton, Jean Cassou, Jean Cayrol, Jean-Marie Domenach, Marguerite Duras, Pierre Emmanuel, André Frénaud, Michel Leiris, Alain Robbe-Grillet and Maurice Nadeau.

"We regret to communicate our concern regarding the fate of Andrei Sinyavsky and Yuli Daniel, arrested in September in Moscow. The damage caused to cultural relations between the U.S.S.R. and France by this arrest of writers whose talents we value, who bring honour to Russian literature, compels us to ask you to use the enormous authority which you enjoy, to demand that the authorities release Sinyavsky and Daniel."

If you wanted to ruin a party, you could have done it no better.

And it's not just the French. Writers from Chile, Mexico, Italy and India bombard him with snivelling messages.

François Mauriac has written a personal letter. So have Arthur Miller, Saul Bellow and Mary McCarthy.

It's so annoying.

Sholokhov does not set foot outside the Grand Hotel in Stockholm anymore, nor does he answer any phone calls that have not been duly filtered beforehand by the

* Mikhail Sholokhov, *Virgin Soil Upturned*, transl. Stephen Garry (Putnam, N.Y., 1941 [reprint]), p. 12, 14, 17

Competent Authority. It's impossible to get his reaction. He is preparing his acceptance speech.

"I should like my books to assist people in becoming better, in becoming purer in their minds; I should like them to arouse love of one's fellow men, a desire to fight actively for the ideal of humanity and the progress of mankind," he declares to the Swedish Academy.

Hello, thanks for the prize, goodbye – he's gone.

Three months later, once Sinyavsky and Daniel are sentenced, from the tribune of the Twenty-Third Party Congress, he will at last express the real source of his irritation:

"If those little hoodlums with their dark souls had been caught in the 1920s, when criminals were judged, not according to the well-defined Articles of the Criminal Code, but guided by one's revolutionary conscience... Believe me, those ruffians would not have received that lenient punishment!"

Because they tainted his Nobel Prize and his champagne, he could just see himself wielding a Nagant revolver, giving them a literary award of his own, with feeling, in the back of their heads.

Vysotsky drops in on Rozanova the day after the arrest. He cheers the family up by bellowing out a song – what else could he do? Except get trashed in solidarity. Rozanova warns him that the recordings of his songs have been seized. The Competent Authority is surely dissecting them now.

"The shitstorm's only just starting," Vysotsky supposes.

Captain Nikonovich, in fact, has taken charge of the tapes. He listens to them, again and again and again… That hoarse voice, so human, so warm and sincere, does have an impact on him, without a doubt. It's the complete opposite of your typical official singer you see on the television with a lamp post stuck up his arse, in a suit and tie as stiff as a coffin, backed by a gaggle of musicians sitting in rows two by two.

He puts the tapes away in a drawer, under a pile of papers. In a little while, he'll appropriate them on the sly – that's the rascal's plan for them.

That's forgetting Rozanova. Once the investigation is complete, she demands that everything be returned to her. Three tapes by Vysotsky were confiscated, three should be returned! Where are they? Lost? Are you shitting me? The Competent Authority admits, bashfully, that they have no idea where they are.

Rozanova, with a cannibal smile, threatens to distribute a statement saying she was robbed during the search.

The officers wince a bit and declare that they do not like being spoken to in that tone. They remind Rozanova that they can arrest her too at any moment for conspiracy.

"Iegor will then go to an orphanage," Pakhmonov says.

"I dare you."

She lays a list down on the investigator's desk, with the names of thirty foreign journalists who are waiting only for a sign from her to distribute an abominable declaration to the effect that the regime, not satisfied with imprisoning a writer, is also persecuting his wife and child.

"I've seen to everything," she lies. "This statement is already in Paris, with Hélène Peltier."

While the investigator is pouring himself a few drops of valerian onto a sugar cube, Rozanova continues, all honey:

"We would both have a lot to lose, don't you think? What would your superiors say? What's the point of going to war with us? I am within my rights. Give me back my tapes."

Easier said than done.

Once Rozanova has left, a search is conducted, a frenzied excavation.

"It's a good opportunity to do some spring cleaning," Pakhmonov says to motivate himself.

The wretched tapes finally turn up in the possession of Captain Nikonovich. He earns himself a memorable nuclear explosion from Colonel Volkov. His request for a transfer to the provinces will be accepted. He'll end up disappearing into the masses.

Ivanov attends the trial, accompanied by Kulakov and twenty or so operatives in plain clothes, packing the little courtroom to stop just anyone from getting in. A pointless precaution, since you have to have an official pass anyway, duly certified by the higher powers.

There's Rozanova, sitting in the first row, taking notes. She turns around, sees Ivanov, gives him a little wave. Ivanov doesn't know where to put himself, it's so embarrassing, this familiarity.

And there are the two accused, relaxed, sitting in the dock. They look like two classmates saying hello again on the first day of school. "So, what did you get up to on your summer holidays?" "No, no, you go first, you tell me."

They are no longer denying that they are Tertz and Arzhak – they quickly admitted that during the investigation. Yes, they wrote those incriminating texts, yes, they passed them to the West, yes, they are happy to be published over there, even if they would rather be published in their own country.

Published in their own country? Whatever next? Do they expect to get the Lenin prize or something, those good-for-nothings who have never hammered in a nail or milked a cow in their life?

No regrets, no shadows disturb their statements.

They persist in denying the evidence. They say their writings are not anti-Soviet. Come on now. Ivanov is outraged: you just have to see the mountain of letters of support, articles and broadcasts from capitalist countries accumulating on his desk, to understand which camp they're in. Tell me who your friends are, I'll tell you who you are.

They pretend not to understand. Their passages about Lenin and the moon, about the public murder day are read aloud to the court – this just makes them smile.

With their calm, their detachment, they look as though they're making fun of the judges, and, by extension, of the entire Soviet population.

"The arguments of the prosecution have not convinced me, I stand by my position," Sinyavsky says. "In my opinion, it is impossible to subject a literary text to a judicial enquiry. It seems to me that you know this, but that you are ignoring it on purpose, because you need to concoct an enemy for yourselves at any price. I plead not guilty."

This man, who was so frightened at his arrest, behaves in prison like a flower that has just been watered. His leaves have perked up, an insolent serenity seems to radiate from him. Whence does he drink this vivifying sap? It's not that he's making light of the situation, let's not go that far, but you do get the sense that he is in his natural element at last.

Sinyavsky might as well be a form of lichen. With his bushy beard, his crossed eyes and the steady elocution of a university professor, he'd be capable of adapting to lunar soil if you gave him half the chance.

It almost makes you wonder whether Sinyavsky would be disappointed if he was acquitted – but that's never going to happen.

The verdict is handed down: seven years of hard labour in a prison camp for Sinyavsky, five for Daniel.

Thus has justice been served.

XXII

Smiling even wider than ever, Rozanova welcomes Ivanov.
"Do come in, lieutenant, make yourself at home!"
"Captain. I'm a captain now."
"A captain already?"
"I mean, I'm not here on a, um… It's not to… It's a friendly visit, so to speak. First to tell you that your husband is doing well, and is in good health."
Why does this woman have to make him feel so ill at ease?
"I never doubted it. It's in our common interest that nothing should happen to him, isn't it? And, just between you and me, I'm happy that he's there with you, well guarded, in Mordovia. Because you never know, with husbands, do you, they can always fly away to other skies. Whereas there, with you, for seven years, there's no risk. How's the health of our Lieutenant-Colonel Pakhmonov, extension number 28-17? Is his blood pressure under control? What about Captain Nikonovich?"
This fearsome woman has remembered the names of all the operatives present at the search. And how on earth did she get hold of the number of the investigator's direct line? That's classified Confidential! Ivanov has a shiver of

irrationality. He gets the sense that she's the kind of person who knows that the "M" on his Erica now jams a bit when you type too fast.

"Nikonovich is no longer working with us. I mean, not in our team."

"Why? Did he do something stupid? And you've changed glasses, haven't you? Look, while you're here, give me a hand with this box of books, would you? They need to be put back up on that shelf. Watch the ceiling light! And don't wreck your microphones!"

"Maria Vasilyevna!" Ivanov sighs, balancing up on a stool. "The operational constraint is over. You know very well there are no more listening devices in your home."

He is offended that anyone would suspect the Competent Authority of not playing fair.

"What about that white thing, over there, along the pipe?" she asks. "I mean, you can hardly see it, but still…"

That's not a good look. Those slobs from the operations team forgot a wire. That's no way to do your job now, is it?

"Mind you, I'm not complaining. Record me all you like if it gives you a thrill. I'm an ordinary woman, I have nothing to hide. Like all citizens of the Soviet Union."

Ordinary, she certainly isn't, Ivanov thinks. And "woman"? You must be joking! More like a boa constrictor!

He can't stay forever.

"Maria Vasilyevna, I've also come to give you a message. Why don't you get Andrei Donatovich to sign a request for early release for good conduct?"

He explains that this request, if it is written correctly, would have every chance of being favourably considered by those it may concern. Her husband is a writer, after all, not a speculator. He hints that the Competent Authority has had enough of this campaign in support of Sinyavsky, which is still splashed over all the Western newspapers. If he were granted early release, it would be a win–win situation for everyone, wouldn't it?

"I beg you, Maria Vasilyevna, don't let him rot away down there. Because of his obstinacy in pleading not guilty, his file has been stamped 'to be employed in the most demanding work'. He's on the night shift, loading and unloading train cars. Wood, coal… It's not good… His health… We know you are a positive influence on him."

He feels awkward, just like when he was proposing to Larissa.

"It's tempting," Rozanova considers. "But he may just dig his heels in. He can be very stubborn, my husband can. Like all of you males of the species. To convince him… Would I be allowed a visit?"

Captain Ivanov is delighted.

"A visit? Why of course, let's make it happen!"

"A visit of three days. The maximum allowed, in other words. In the meeting cabin. And without the guard getting an eyeful through the keyhole. I would like you to give me your solemn word on that point. The orders must be clear. It's dreadful, really! Imagine someone ogling you, I mean you and your wife, while you're, you know… What's her name again?"

"Tamara," Ivanov ad libs.

For goodness' sake, the boa constrictor has no business knowing about his private life!

Rozanova is surprised:

"That's funny, I thought it was Larissa. You haven't gone

and changed wives, have you? Thrown off the old one to take a new one, you, a real communist!"

Quick! Change the subject!

Ah, here's Iegor. My, how he's grown!

Ivanov takes out an envelope.

"Here you go, buddy, this is for you. They're stamps. Do you collect stamps? When I was a boy, everyone collected stamps. This block was issued for the fifty-year anniversary of the Competent Authority. The dates are given here: 1917–1967. I got you a sheet of a hundred of them. At the office we have as many as we want."

He rummages in his bag as well, and pulls out a little package wrapped in newspaper.

"I think it was your birthday a few days ago. I thought…"

It was actually Larissa's idea. "The Competent Authority was there when the kid was born. He's a bit like your mascot. Give him a toy. One day, maybe we'll have a boy too…"

A little turquoise car. He found it at Voentorg. Made in the U.S.S.R., there's no way to get it to roll properly. The wheels seize up after three turns.

"It's a ZIL III-V," Ivanov gushes nevertheless. "It was in this limousine, on April 14, 1961, that Gagarin arrived at the Kremlin."

Iegor is puzzled:

"I'm not sure what I can use it for. I already have a toy car that works a lot better. Maybe for spare parts?"

Not a thank you, not a smile. That child is spoilt rotten. Unless he has already been infected by class contempt, the disdain of intellectuals for simple folk. What a family!

"When you've got to go, you've got to go," Ivanov says

as he takes his leave. "Maria Vasilyevna, I'm very happy about our mutual understanding."

He escapes – Rozanova doesn't have time to ask him to shift another box of books.

The following week, she gets off the train at Potma station, in Mordovia. There's an hourly shuttle truck from there that makes all the stops along the route. Twenty-three miles on, she gets off at the stop for "Yavas, colony no. 385".

The meeting cabin is theirs for three whole days. A bed, two chairs, a little table, and a lightbulb to illuminate all this luxury, even at night. The tiny window has curtains of perfectly transparent white. It doesn't open and looks out onto a wall. Everything is handmade out of wood, with a saw, the local production of the *zeks* themselves.

Ivanov kept his word: there are no voyeurs at the keyholes. Alone at last!

The first thing Sinyavsky says is:

"My God, Masha! You have no idea how fascinating this place is!"

His crossed eyes sparkle.

"All these *zeks*, all this humanity!"

Then he comes back down to earth and points cunningly at the floor – careful! An experienced prison mate warned him. Rozanova understands at once. If you stick your ear to the gunge on the floor, you can hear the motor of a tape deck hissing – they are being recorded. Every hour it goes clack! Change the reel!

And so, before throwing themselves at each other to sate their hunger, the couple exchange news from the front in an improvised sign language.

"There's no way I will ask for early release," Sinyavsky

raises his eyebrows. "That would amount to recognising that I'm guilty. Don't you agree?"

Rozanova giggles.

"Of course I do! But if you pretend to hesitate, and I pretend to try and convince you, we have some leverage and room to manoeuvre. The guys at the Competent Authority are just like everyone else, they run on hope. And we…"

She makes an obscene gesture.

"We'll fuck with them."

"We'll fuck with them so we can fuck."

Neither the clack! of the reel, nor the stench of old tobacco permeating the blankets, nor the guards' noisy conversations and footsteps so close by, nor even their own weariness, their almost complete exhaustion – nothing can hold back the adventurers.

Evgeny Fyodorovich Ivanov climbed up the ranks of the Competent Authority to become a general. Viewed favourably in the upper echelons for his faithfulness to the Party, at ease in the swamps of the bureaucracy, he finally ended up as the head of the famous fifth directorate (chasing dissidents) created by Yuri Andropov in the wake of the Sinyavsky–Daniel affair. He carried out several missions in France, where he was identified as one of the "diplomats" and expelled in 1983. After the collapse of the U.S.S.R., he worked on the staff of media oligarch Vladimir Gusinsky. He is a member of honour of the veteran club of the Cheka–K.G.B–F.S.B.

In recompense for services rendered, "Monocle" was sent abroad to Dresden, a city where no-one knew of his past as a *seksot*. He spent the rest of his days there, teaching the history and architecture of Central Asia.

The torch at Urta-Bulak burned for two years and ten months. It was indeed snuffed out by the underground explosion of a nuclear device, on September 30, 1966.

Andrei Sinyavsky was released in June 1971, after five years and nine months of imprisonment. In 1973, he was allowed to emigrate to France with his family, where he became a professor of Russian literature at the Sorbonne.

ACKNOWLEDGEMENTS

It would be overlong to cite all the sources used here. However, these are a few of the works that have been faithful companions:

Le Livre blanc du procès Siniavski–Daniel, compiled by Alexandre Guinzburg, Posev, 1967.

On Trial: the case of Sinyavsky (Tertz) and Daniel (Arzhak): documents, by Leopold Labedz and Max Hayward, Harvill Press, London, 1967.

Goodnight: a novel, by Abram Tertz (Andrei Sinyavsky), Penguin, 1991.

The Road to Australia, by Vladimir Kabo, Aboriginal Studies Press, 1998.

The Apparatus of the Central Committee of the C.P.S.U. and Culture (1965–1972): documents, compiled by N.G. Tomilina et al., Rosspen, 2009 (in Russian, untranslated).

Daily Life in the Soviet Capital under Khrushchev and Brezhnev, by Aleksandr A. Vaskin, Molodaya Gvardia, 2018 (in Russian, untranslated).

Life Turned Out To Be Long, by Lyudmila G. Sergeeva, AST, 2019 (in Russian, untranslated).

I wish to particularly thank the Hoover Institution in Stanford, California, where the archives of Andrei Sinyavsky are preserved.

I take my hat off to that handful of Soviet intellectuals who dared publicly to protest against the Sinyavsky–Daniel trial, many of whom were subjected to calumny, expulsions and other persecutions. Finally, I salute these devoted friends, who did so much on a daily basis to ensure our survival: Emma Shitova, Lazar Fleishman, Igor Golomstock, Vilya Khoslavskaya, Emile Liuboshitz, Andrei and Lydia Menshutin, Evgeny Rosenblum, Lyudmila Sergeeva.